A TR

(A KE

BLAKE PIERCE

ISBN: 978-1-63291-928-1

BOOKS BY BLAKE PIERCE

RILEY PAIGE MYSTERY SERIES
ONCE GONE (Book #1)
ONCE TAKEN (Book #2)
ONCE CRAVED (Book #3)
ONCE LURED (Book #4)
ONCE HUNTED (Book #5)
ONCE PINED (Book #6)

MACKENZIE WHITE MYSTERY SERIES
BEFORE HE KILLS (Book #1)
BEFORE HE SEES (Book #2)
BEFORE HE COVETS (Book #3)

AVERY BLACK MYSTERY SERIES
CAUSE TO KILL (Book #1)
CAUSE TO RUN (Book #2)
CAUSE TO HIDE (Book #3)

KERI LOCKE MYSTERY SERIES
A TRACE OF DEATH (Book #1)

PROLOGUE

He glanced at his watch.

2:59 PM.

The school bell would ring in less than a minute.

Ashley only lived about twelve blocks from the high school, less than a mile, and almost always made the trek alone. That was his only concern—that today would be one of the rare occasions where she had company.

Within five minutes of school letting out, she was in sight, and his heart sank as he saw her walking with two other girls along Main Street. They stopped at an intersection and chatted. This wouldn't do. They had to leave her. They *had* to.

He felt the anxiety rise in his belly. This was supposed to be the day.

Sitting in the front seat of his van, he tried to control what he liked to call his *original self*. It was his original self which emerged when he was doing his special experiments on his specimens back at home. It was his original self which allowed him to ignore the screams and begging of those specimens so he could focus on his important work.

He had to keep his original self well hidden. He reminded himself to call them girls and not specimens. He reminded himself to use proper names like "Ashley." He reminded himself that to other people, he looked completely normal and that if he acted that way, no one could tell what lurked in his heart.

He'd been doing it for years, acting normal. Some people even called him *smooth*. He liked that. It meant he was a great actor. And by acting normal almost all the time, he'd somehow carved out a life, one that some might even envy. He could hide in plain sight.

Yet now he could feel it bursting in his chest, begging to be let free. The desire was getting the better of him—he had to rein it in.

He closed his eyes and took several deep breaths, trying to remember the instructions. On the last breath, he inhaled for five seconds and then exhaled slowly, allowing the noise he'd learned to escape his mouth slowly.

"Ohhhmmm…"

He opened his eyes—and felt a rush of relief. Her two friends had turned west on Clubhouse Avenue toward the water. Ashley continued south on Main Street alone, next to the dog park.

Some afternoons she lingered there, watching dogs tear across the wood chip–covered ground after tennis balls. But not today. Today, she walked with purpose, as if she had somewhere to be.

If she'd known what was coming, she wouldn't have bothered.

That thought made him smile to himself.

He'd always thought she was attractive. And as he inched his way along the street behind her, making sure to give way to the cavalcade of high school jaywalkers, he once again admired her lean, athletic surfer's body. She was wearing a pink skirt that stopped just above the knees and a bright blue top that hugged her close.

He made his move.

A warm calmness washed over him. He activated the unconventional-looking e-cigarette that had been resting on the van's center console and pressed his foot gently on the gas pedal.

He pulled up next to her in the van and called out through the open passenger window.

"Hey."

At first she looked taken aback. She squinted into the vehicle, clearly unable to tell who it was.

"It's me," he said casually. He put the van in park, leaned over, and opened the passenger door so she could see who it was.

She leaned in a little to get a better look. After a moment, he saw something like recognition cross her face.

"Oh, hi. Sorry," she apologized.

"No problem," he assured her, before taking a long drag.

She looked more closely at the device in his hand.

"I've never seen one like that before."

"You want to check it out?" he offered as casually as he could.

She nodded and stepped closer, leaning in. He leaned toward her as well, as if he were about to take it out of his mouth and hand it to her. But when she was about three feet away, he clicked a little button on the device, which made a small clasp open, and which sprayed a chemical right for her face, in a small fog. At the same moment, he raised a mask to his own nose, so as not to breathe it himself.

It was so subtle and quiet that Ashley didn't even notice. Before she could react, her eyes began to close, her body to slump.

She was already leaning forward, losing consciousness, and all he had to do was reach over and ease her into the passenger seat. To the casual observer, it might even look like she got in of her own accord.

His heart was thumping but he reminded himself to stay calm. He had come this far.

He reached across the specimen, pulled the passenger door closed, and properly secured her seatbelt and then his own. Finally, he allowed himself one last slow deep breath in and out.

When he was sure the coast was clear, he edged out into the street.

Soon he merged with the mid-afternoon Southern California traffic, just another commuter blending in, trying to navigate his way in a sea of humanity.

CHAPTER ONE

Monday
Late Afternoon

Detective Keri Locke pleaded with herself not to do it this time. As the most junior detective in the West Los Angeles Pacific Division Missing Persons Unit, she was expected to work harder than anyone else in the division. And as a thirty-five-year-old woman who'd only joined the force four years ago, she often felt like she was supposed to be the hardest-working cop in the entire LAPD. She couldn't afford to look like she was taking a break.

All around her, the department buzzed with activity. An elderly Hispanic woman was sitting at a nearby desk, giving a statement about a purse snatching. Down the hall, a carjacker was being booked. It was a typical afternoon in what had become her new normal of a life. And yet that recurring urge was eating at her, refusing to be ignored.

She gave in to it. She stood up and wandered over to the window that looked out on Culver Boulevard. She stood there and could nearly see her reflection. With the dancing glare from the afternoon sun, she looked part human, part ghost.

That was how she felt. She knew that objectively, she was an attractive woman. Five foot six and about 130 pounds—133 if she was being honest—with dirty blonde hair and a figure that had escaped childbirth relatively unscathed, she still turned heads.

But if anyone looked closely, they'd see that her brown eyes were red and bleary, her forehead was a knotted mass of premature lines, and her skin often had the pallor of, well, a ghost.

Like most days, she was wearing a simple blouse tucked into black slacks and black flats that looked professional but were easy to run in. Her hair was pulled back in a ponytail. It was her unofficial uniform. Pretty much the only thing that changed daily was the color of the top she wore. It all reinforced her feeling that she was marking time more than really living.

Keri sensed movement out of the corner of her eye and snapped out of her reverie. They were coming.

Outside the window, Culver Boulevard was mostly devoid of people. There was a running and biking path across the street. On most days in the late afternoon, it was choked with foot traffic. But it was relentlessly hot today, with temperatures in the high nineties and no breeze at all, even here, less than five miles from the beach.

4

Parents who normally walked their kids home from school took their air-conditioned cars today. Except for one.

At exactly 4:12, just like clockwork, a young girl on a bike, about seven or eight years old, pedaled slowly down the path. She wore a fancy white dress. Her youngish mom trailed behind her in jeans and a T-shirt, with a backpack slung casually over her shoulder.

Keri fought the anxiety bubbling in her stomach and looked around to see if anyone in the office was watching her. No one was. She allowed herself to give in to the itch she'd tried not to scratch all day and stared.

Keri watched them with jealous, adoring eyes. She still couldn't believe it, even after so many times at this window. The girl was the spitting image of Evie, right down to the wavy blond hair, the green eyes, even the slightly crooked smile.

She stood there in a trance, staring out the window long after the mother and child had disappeared from sight.

When she finally snapped out of it and turned back to the bullpen, the elderly Hispanic woman was leaving. The carjacker had been processed. Some new miscreant, cuffed and surly, had slid into his spot at the booking window, an alert uniformed officer standing at his left elbow.

She glanced up at the digital clock on the wall above the coffee machine. It read 4:22.

Have I really been standing at that window for ten solid minutes? This is getting worse, not better.

She walked back to her desk with her head down, trying not to make eye contact with any curious co-workers. She sat and looked at the files on her desk. The Martine case was largely wrapped up, just waiting for a sign-off from the prosecutor before she could dump it in the "complete until trial" cabinet. The Sanders case was on hold until CSU came back with its preliminary report. Rampart division had asked Pacific to look into a prostitute named Roxie who had dropped off the radar; a co-worker had told them she'd started working the Westside and they were hoping someone in her unit could confirm that so they didn't have to open a file.

The tricky thing with missing persons cases, at least for adults, was that it wasn't a crime to disappear. Police had more leeway with minors, depending on the age. But in general, there was nothing to prevent people from simply dropping out of their lives. It happened more often than most people would expect. Without some evidence of foul play, law enforcement was limited in what they could legally do to investigate. Because of that, cases like Roxie's often fell through the cracks in the system.

Sighing in resignation, Keri realized that barring something extraordinary, there was really no reason to stick around beyond five.

She closed her eyes and pictured herself, less than an hour from now, kicking back on her houseboat, *Sea Cups*, pouring herself three fingers—okay, four—of Glenlivet and settling in to an evening of leftover Chinese takeout and a few reruns of *Scandal*. If that personalized therapy didn't pan out, she might end up back on Dr. Blanc's couch, an unappealing alternative.

She had started to pack up her files for the day when Ray walked in and plopped himself in the chair across the large desk they shared. Ray was officially Detective Raymond "Big" Sands, her partner of nearly a year now and her friend for closer to seven.

He matched his nickname in every way. Ray (Keri never called him "Big"—he didn't need the ego stroking) was a six-foot-four, 230-pound black guy with a shiny bald head, a chipped lower tooth, a meticulously trimmed goatee, and a penchant for wearing dress shirts a size too small for him, just to emphasize his build.

Forty years old now, Ray still resembled the bronze-medal-winning Olympic boxer he'd been at age twenty and the professional heavyweight contender, with a record of 28-2-1, he'd been until the age of twenty-eight. That was when a scrappy little southpaw five inches shorter than him took out his right eye with a vicious hook and brought everything to a screeching halt. He wore a patch for two years afterward, didn't like the discomfort, and finally got a glass eye, which somehow worked for him.

Like Keri, Ray joined the Force later than most, when he was searching for a new purpose in his early thirties. He rose through the ranks quickly and was now the senior detective in Pacific Division's Missing Persons Unit, or MPU.

"You look like a woman dreaming of waves and whiskey," he said.

"Is it that obvious?" Keri asked.

"I'm a good detective. My powers of observation are unmatched. Also, you mentioned your exciting evening plans twice today already."

"What can I say? I'm dogged in pursuit of my goals, Raymond."

He smiled, his one good eye betraying a warmth his physical demeanor hid. Keri was the only one allowed to call him by his proper name. She liked to mix it up with other, less flattering, titles. He often did the same to her.

6

"Listen, Little Miss Sunshine, maybe you'd be better off spending the last few minutes of your shift checking in with CSU on the Sanders case instead of daydreaming about day drinking."

"Day drinking?" she said, mock offended. "It's not day drinking if I start after five, Gigantor."

He was about to come back at her when the line rang. Keri picked up before Ray could say anything and stuck her tongue out at him playfully.

"Pacific Division Missing Persons. Detective Locke speaking."

Ray got on the line as well but didn't talk.

The woman on the phone sounded young, late twenties or early thirties. Before she even said why she was calling, Keri noted the worry in her voice.

"My name is Mia Penn. I live off Dell Avenue in the Venice Canals. I'm worried about my daughter, Ashley. She should have been home from school by three thirty. She knew I was taking her to a four forty-five dentist appointment. She texted me just before she left school at three but she's not here and she's not responding to any of my calls or texts. This isn't like her at all. She's very responsible."

"Ms. Penn, does Ashley usually drive or walk home?" Keri asked.

"She walks. She's only in tenth grade—she's fifteen. She hasn't even started Driver's Ed yet."

Keri looked at Ray. She knew what he was going to say and she couldn't really argue the point. But something in Mia Penn's tone got to her. She could tell the woman was barely holding it together. There was panic just below the surface. She wanted to ask him to dispense with protocol but couldn't come up with a credible reason why.

"Ms. Penn, this is Detective Ray Sands. I'm conferencing in. I want you to take a deep breath and then tell me if your daughter's ever been home late before."

Mia Penn launched in, forgetting the deep breath part.

"Of course," she admitted, trying to hide the exasperation in her voice. "Like I said, she's fifteen. But she's always texted or called if she wasn't back within an hour or so. And never if we had plans."

Ray responded without glancing at what he knew would be Keri's disapproving glare.

"Ms. Penn, officially, your daughter is a minor and so typical missing person laws don't apply as they would for an adult. We have broader authority to investigate. But speaking to you honestly, a teenage girl who isn't responding to her mother's texts and isn't home less than two hours after school lets out— that's not going to command the kind of immediate response you're hoping for. At this point there's not much we can do. In a situation like this, your best bet is to come down to the station and file a report. You should absolutely do that. There's no harm in it and it could expedite things if we need to ramp up resources."

There was a long pause before Mia Penn responded. Her voice had a sharp edge that wasn't there before.

"How long do I have to wait before you 'ramp up,' Detective?" she demanded. "Is two more hours enough? Do I have to wait until it gets dark? Until she's not home in the morning? I'll bet that if I was—"

Whatever Mia Penn was about to say, she stopped herself, as if she knew that anything else she added would be counterproductive. Ray was about to respond but Keri held up her hand and gave him her patented "let me handle this" look.

"Listen, Ms. Penn, this is Detective Locke again. You said you live in the Canals, right? That's on my way home. Give me your e-mail address. I'll send you the missing persons form. You can get started on it and I'll stop by to help you finish it up and expedite getting it in the system. How does that sound?"

"It sounds good, Detective Locke. Thank you."

"No problem. And hey, maybe Ashley will be home by the time I get there and I can give her a stern lecture on keeping her mom better informed—free of charge."

Keri gathered her purse and keys, preparing to head to the Penn house.

Ray hadn't said a word since they'd hung up. She knew he was silently seething but she refused to look up. If he caught her eye, then *she'd* be the one getting the lecture and she wasn't in the mood.

But Ray apparently didn't need to make eye contact to say his piece.

"The Canals are *not* on your way home."

"They're only a little out of my way," she insisted, still not looking up. "So I'll have to wait until six thirty to get back to the marina and Olivia Pope and associates. No big deal."

Ray exhaled and leaned back in his chair.

"It *is* a big deal. Keri, you've been a detective here almost a year now. I like having you as my partner. And you've done some great work, even before you got your shield. The Gonzales case, for example. I don't think I could have solved that one and I've been investigating these cases for a decade longer than you. You have a kind of sixth sense about these things. That's why we used you as a resource in the old days. And it's why you have the potential to be a truly great detective."

"Thanks," she said, though she knew he wasn't finished.

"But you have one major weakness and it's going to ruin you if you don't get a handle on it. You have got to let the system work. It's here for a reason. Seventy-five percent of our job will work itself out in the first twenty-four hours without our help. We need to let that happen and concentrate on the other twenty-five percent. If we don't, we end up running ourselves ragged. We become unproductive, or worse—counterproductive. And then we're betraying the people who really end up needing us. It's part of our job to choose our battles."

"Ray, I'm not ordering an Amber Alert or anything. I'm just helping a worried mother fill out some paperwork. And truly, it's only fifteen minutes out of my way."

"And…" he said expectantly.

"*And* there was something in her voice. She's holding something back. I just want to talk to her face to face. It might be nothing. And if it is, I'll leave."

Ray shook his head and tried one more time.

"How many hours did you waste on that homeless kid in Palms you were certain had gone missing but hadn't? Fifteen?"

Keri shrugged.

"Better safe than sorry," she muttered under her breath.

"Better employed than discharged for inappropriate use of department resources," he countered.

"It's after five," Keri said.

"Meaning?"

"Meaning I'm off the clock. And that mother is waiting for me."

"It would appear that you're never off the clock. Call her back, Keri. Tell her to e-mail the forms back when she's done. Tell her to call here if she has any questions. But go home."

She'd been as patient as she could but as far as she was concerned, the conversation was over.

"I'll see you tomorrow, Mr. Clean," she said, giving him a squeeze on the arm.

As she headed for the parking lot and her ten-year-old silver Toyota Prius, she tried to remember the quickest shortcut to the Venice Canals. She already felt an urgency she didn't understand.

One she didn't like.

CHAPTER TWO

Monday
Late Afternoon

Keri threaded the Prius through rush hour traffic to the western edge of Venice, driving faster than she meant to. Something was driving her, a gut feeling rising up, one she didn't like.

The Canals were only a few blocks from tourist hot spots like the Boardwalk and Muscle Beach and it took ten minutes of driving up and down Pacific Avenue before she finally found a spot to park. She hopped out and let her phone direct her the rest of the way on foot.

The Venice Canals weren't just a name for a neighborhood. They were a real series of man-made canals built in the early twentieth century, and modeled after the originals in Italy. They covered about ten square blocks just south of Venice Boulevard. A few of the homes that lined the waterways were modest, but most were extravagant in a beachy way. The lots were generally small but some of the homes were easily worth eight figures.

The one Keri arrived at was among the most impressive. It was three stories high, and only the top floor was visible due to the high stucco wall that surrounded it. She walked around from the back, which faced the canal, to the front door. As she did, she noticed multiple security cameras on the mansion walls and the house itself. Several of them seemed to be tracking her movements.

Why does a twenty-something mom with a teenage daughter live here? And why such heavy security?

She reached the wrought-iron gate in front and was surprised to find it open. She stepped through and was about to knock on the front door when it opened from the inside.

A woman stepped out to meet her, wearing frayed jeans and a white tank top, with long, thick brown hair and bare feet. As Keri suspected from hearing her on the phone, she couldn't have been more than thirty. About Keri's height and easily twenty pounds lighter, she was tanned and fit. And she was gorgeous, despite the anxious expression on her face.

Keri's first thought was *trophy wife.*

"Mia Penn?" Keri asked.

"Yes. Please come in, Detective Locke. I've already filled out the forms you sent."

Inside, the mansion opened into a commanding foyer, with two matching marble staircases leading to an upper level. There was

10

almost enough room to play a Lakers game. The interior was immaculate, with art covering every wall and sculptures adorning carved wooden tables that looked like they might be art as well.

The whole place looked like it could be featured on a moment's notice in *Homes That Make You Question Your Self-Worth* magazine. Keri recognized one prominently placed painting as a Delano, meaning that all by itself, it was worth more than the pathetic twenty-year-old houseboat she called home.

Mia Penn guided her to one of the more casual living rooms and offered her a seat and a bottled water. In the corner of the room, a thickly built man in slacks and a sport jacket leaned casually against the wall. He didn't say anything but his eyes never left Keri. She noticed a small bulge on his right hip under the jacket.

Gun. Must be security.

Once Keri sat, her hostess didn't waste any time.

"Ashley's still not answering my calls or texts. She hasn't tweeted since school let out. No new Facebook posts. Nothing on Instagram." She exhaled and added, "Thanks for coming. I can't even begin to tell you how much this means to me."

Keri nodded slowly, studying Mia Penn, trying to get a sense of her. Just as on the phone, the barely concealed panic felt real.

She seems to genuinely fear for her daughter. But she's holding something back.

"You're younger than I expected," Keri finally said.

"I'm thirty. I had Ashley when I was fifteen."

"Wow."

"Yeah, that's pretty much what everyone says. I feel like because we're so close in age, we have this connection. I swear sometimes I know what she's feeling even before I see her. I know it sounds ridiculous but we have this bond. And I know it's not evidence but I can *feel* that something's wrong."

"Let's not panic quite yet," Keri said.

They went over the facts.

The last time Mia saw Ashley was that morning. Everything was fine. She had yogurt with granola and sliced strawberries for breakfast. She'd left for school in a good mood.

Ashley's best friend was Thelma Gray. Mia called her when Ashley didn't show up after school. According to Thelma, Ashley was in third-period geometry like she was supposed to be and everything seemed normal. The last time she saw Ashley was in the hall around 2 PM. She had no idea why Ashley didn't make it home.

Mia had also spoken to Ashley's boyfriend, a jock-type named Denton Rivers. He said he saw Ashley in school in the morning but that was it. He texted her a few times after school but she never answered.

Ashley didn't take any medications; she had no physical ailments to speak of. Mia said she'd gone through Ashley's room earlier in the afternoon and everything was normal.

Keri scribbled it all down on a little pad, making specific note of names she'd follow up with later.

"My husband should be home from the office any minute. I know he wants to speak with you as well."

Keri looked up from her pad. Something in Mia's voice had changed. It sounded more guarded, cautious.

Whatever she's hiding, I bet it's related to this.

"And what's your husband's name?" she asked, trying to keep it light.

"His name's Stafford."

"Wait a minute," Keri said. "Your husband is *Stafford Penn*, as in *United States Senator Stafford Penn*?"

"Yes."

"That's kind of important information, Mrs. Penn. Why didn't you mention it before?"

"Stafford asked me not to," she said apologetically.

"Why?"

"He said he'd like to address that with you when he arrived."

"When did you say he'd be here again?"

"Less than ten minutes, for sure."

Keri looked at her hard, trying to decide whether to push. Ultimately, she chose to hold off for now.

"Do you have a picture of Ashley?"

Mia Penn handed over her phone. The background photo was of a teenage girl in a sundress. She looked like Mia's younger sister. Other than Ashley having blonde hair, they were hard to tell apart. Ashley was slightly taller, with a more athletic frame and a deeper tan. The dress couldn't hide her muscular legs and powerful shoulders. Keri suspected she was a regular surfer.

"Could she just have forgotten about the appointment and be out catching waves?" Keri asked.

Mia smiled for the first time since Keri met her.

"I'm impressed, Detective. You made that guess based on one picture? No, Ashley likes to surf in the mornings—better swells and fewer troublemakers. I checked the garage just in case. Her board's in there."

"Can you send me that photo as well as a few close-ups with and without makeup?"

While Mia did that, Keri asked another question.

"Where does she go to school?"

"West Venice High."

Keri couldn't hide her surprise. She knew the place well. It was a large public high school, a melting pot of thousands of kids, with everything that entailed. She had arrested many a student who attended West Venice.

Why the hell is the wealthy daughter of a US senator going there instead of a fancy private school?

Mia must have read the surprise on Keri's face.

"Stafford's never liked it. He's always wanted her in private schools, on track to Harvard, where he went. But it wasn't just for better academics. He also wanted better security," she said. "I've always wanted her in public schools, to be in the mix of real kids where she could learn about real life. It's one of the few battles I've actually won with him. If Ashley ends up hurt because of something at school, it will be my fault."

Keri wanted to nip that kind of thinking in the bud fast.

"One—Ashley is going to be fine. Two—if anything were to happen to her it would the fault of the person who hurt her, not the mother who loves her."

Keri watched to see if Mia Penn bought it but she couldn't tell. The truth was, her reassurance was intended to keep a valuable resource from falling apart more than to buck her up. She decided to press on.

"Let's talk about that for a second. Is there anyone who would want to hurt her, or you or Stafford, for that matter?"

"Ashley, no; me, no; Stafford, nothing specific that I'm aware of, other than what comes with the territory of doing what he does. I mean he gets death threats from constituents who claim to be aliens. So it's hard to know what to take seriously. "

"And no one's called demanding ransom, right?"

The sudden stress on the woman's face was palpable.

"Is that what you think this is?"

"No, no, no, I'm just covering the bases. I don't think it's anything yet. These are all just routine questions."

"No. There have been no ransom demands."

"You obviously have some money—"

Mia nodded.

"I come from a very wealthy family. But no one really knows that. Everyone assumes our money comes from Stafford."

13

"Out of curiosity, how much are we talking about, exactly?" Keri asked. Sometimes this job made discretion impossible.

"Exactly? I don't know—we have a beachfront house in Miami and a condo in San Francisco, both owned under company names. We're active in the market and have lots of other assets. You've seen all the art in the house. Altogether we're probably talking about fifty-five to sixty million."

"Does Ashley know?"

The woman shrugged.

"To a point—she doesn't know the exact figures but she knows there's a lot of it and that the public isn't supposed to know about all of it. Stafford likes to project a 'man of the people' persona."

"Would she talk about it? Just to her friends, maybe?"

"No. She's under strict instructions not to." The woman exhaled and said, "God, I'm really shooting my mouth off. Stafford would be livid."

"Do you two get along?"

"Yes, of course."

"How about Ashley? Do you get along with her?"

"There's no one in the world I'm closer to."

"Okay. Does Stafford get along with her?"

"They get along fine."

"Is there any reason she'd run away from home?"

"No. Not even close. That's not what's going on here."

"How's her mood been lately?"

"It's been good. She's happy, stable, all of it."

"No boy trouble—"

"No."

"Drugs or alcohol?"

"I can't say never. But in general, she's a responsible young lady. This summer she trained as a junior lifeguard. She had to be up at five in the morning every day for that. She's not a flake. Besides, she hasn't even had time to get bored yet. This is her second week back to school."

"Any drama there?"

"No. She likes her teachers. She gets along with all the kids. She'll be going out for the girls' basketball team."

Keri locked eyes with the woman and asked, "So what do *you* think is going on?"

Confusion washed over the woman's face. Her lips trembled.

"I don't know." She turned her eyes to the front door, then back, and said, "I just want her to come home. Where the hell is Stafford?"

14

As if on cue, a man appeared from around a corner. It was Senator Stafford Penn. Keri had seen him dozens of times on TV. But in person, he gave off a vibe that didn't come through onscreen. About forty-five, he was muscular and tall, easily six foot two, with blond hair like Ashley's, a chiseled jaw, and piercing green eyes. He had a magnetism that seemed to almost vibrate. Keri gulped hard as he extended his hand to shake hers.

"Stafford Penn," he said, although he could tell she already knew that.

Keri smiled.

"Keri Locke," she said. "LAPD Missing Persons Unit, Pacific Division."

Stafford gave his wife a quick peck on the cheek and sat down beside her. He didn't waste any time with pleasantries.

"We appreciate your coming down. But personally, I think we can let it rest until the morning."

Mia looked at him in disbelief.

"Stafford—"

"Kids break away from their parents," he continued. "They wean themselves. It's part of growing up. Hell, if she was a boy, we would have been dealing with days like this two or three years ago. That's why I asked Mia to be discreet when she called you. I doubt this is the last time we'll be dealing with this kind of thing and I don't want to be accused of crying wolf."

Keri asked, "So you don't think anything's wrong?"

He shook his head.

"No. I think she's a teenager doing what teenagers do. To be honest, I'm sort of glad this day has come. It shows she's getting more independent. Mark my words, she'll show up tonight. Worst case, tomorrow morning, probably with a hangover."

Mia stared at him incredulously.

"First of all," she said, "it's a Monday afternoon during the school year, not Spring Break in Daytona. And second, she wouldn't do that."

Stafford shook his head.

"We all get a little crazy sometimes, Mia," he said. "Hell, when I turned fifteen, I drank ten beers in a couple of hours. I was literally heaving my guts out for three days. I remember my dad got a good chuckle out of that. I think he was pretty proud of me, actually."

Keri nodded, pretending that was completely normal. No point in alienating a US senator if she could avoid it.

15

"Thanks, Senator. You're probably right. But as long as I'm here, would you mind if I took a quick peek in Ashley's room?"

He shrugged and pointed to the staircase.

"Go for it."

Upstairs, at the end of the hall, Keri entered Ashley's room and closed the door. The decor was about what she expected—a fancy bed, matching dressers, posters of Adele and one-armed surfing legend Bethany Hamilton. She had a retro lava lamp on the bedside table. Resting on one of her pillows was a stuffed animal. It was so old and tattered that Keri couldn't tell if it was a dog or a sheep.

She fired up the Mac laptop on Ashley's desk and was surprised to find it wasn't password protected.

What teenager leaves her unprotected laptop sitting out on her desk for any nosy adult to check?

The Internet history showed searches for only the last two days; the priors had been cleared. What was left mostly appeared to relate to a biology paper she was researching. There were also a few visits to websites for local modeling agencies, as well as a few in New York and Las Vegas. Another was to the site for an upcoming surfing tournament in Malibu. She had also gone to the site of a local band called Rave.

Either this girl is the most boring goody two-shoes of all time or she's leaving this stuff out on purpose to present an image she wants her folks to buy.

Keri's instinct told her it was the latter.

She sat down at the foot of Ashley's bed and closed her eyes, trying to channel the mindset of a fifteen-year-old girl. She'd been one once. She still hoped to have one of her own. After two minutes, she opened her eyes and tried to look at the room fresh. She scanned the shelves, looking for anything out of the ordinary.

She was about to give up when her gaze fell on a math book at the end of Ashley's bookshelf. It read *Algebra for 9th Grade*.

Didn't Mia say Ashley was in tenth grade? Her friend Thelma saw her in geometry class. *So why is she holding on to an old textbook? Just in case she needs a refresher?*

Keri grabbed the book, opened it, and began paging through it. Two-thirds of the way through, easy to miss, she found two pages carefully taped together. There was something hard in between them.

Keri sliced open part of the tape and something fell out onto the floor. She picked it up. It was an extremely authentic-looking fake driver's license with Ashley's face on it. The name on it was Ashlynn Penner. The date of birth indicated she was twenty-two.

More confident that she was now on the right track, Keri moved quickly through the room. She didn't know how long she had before the Penns got suspicious. After five minutes, she found something else. Tucked in a tennis shoe in the back of the closet was a spent 9mm casing.

She got out an evidence bag, pocketed it along with the fake ID, and left the room. Mia Penn was walking down the hall toward her as she closed the door. Keri could tell something had happened.

"I just got a call from Ashley's friend Thelma. She's been talking to people about Ashley not making it home. She says another friend named Miranda Sanchez saw Ashley get into a black van on Main Street next to a dog park near the school. She said she couldn't be sure if Ashley got in on her own or if she was pulled in. It didn't seem that weird to her until she heard Ashley was missing."

Kerry kept her expression neutral despite the sudden increase in her blood pressure.

"Do you know anyone who has a black van?"

"No one."

Keri started briskly down the hall toward the stairs. Mia Penn tried desperately to keep up.

"Mia, I need you to call the detectives' line at the station—the one you reached me on. Tell whoever picks up—it'll probably be a guy named Suarez—that I said to call. Give him Ashley's physical description and what she was wearing. Also give him the names and contact information for everyone you mentioned to me: Thelma, Miranda, the boyfriend Denton Rivers, all of them. Then tell him to call me."

"Why do you need all that info?"

"We're going to have them all interviewed."

"You're starting to freak me out. This is bad, isn't it?" Mia demanded.

"Probably not. But better safe than sorry."

"What can I do?"

"I need you to stay here in case Ashley calls or shows up."

They got downstairs. Keri looked around.

"Where's your husband?"

"He got called back into work."

Keri bit her tongue and headed for the front door.

"Where are you going?" Mia shouted after her.

Over her shoulder Keri called back:

"I'm going to find your daughter."

CHAPTER THREE

Monday
Early Evening

Outside, as she hurried back to the car, Keri tried to ignore the heat reflecting off the sidewalk. Beads of sweat formed on her brow after only a minute. As she dialed Ray's number, she cursed quietly to herself.

I'm frickin' six blocks from the Pacific Ocean in mid-September. When is this going to let up?

After seven rings, Ray finally picked up.

"What?" he demanded, sounding winded and annoyed.

"I need you to meet me on Main, across from West Venice High."

"When?"

"*Now,* Raymond."

"Hold on a second." She could hear him moving around and muttering under his breath. It didn't sound like he was alone. When he got back on the line, she could tell he'd changed rooms.

"I was kind of otherwise engaged, Keri."

"Well, disengage yourself, Detective. We've got a case."

"Is this that Venice thing?" he asked, clearly exasperated.

"It is. And could you please cut it with the tone. That is, unless you think the daughter of a US senator disappearing into a black van isn't worth checking out."

"Jesus. Why didn't the mother mention the senator thing on the phone?"

"Because he asked her not to. He was as dismissive as you, maybe even more so. Hold on a second."

Keri had reached her car. She put the phone on speaker, tossed it in the passenger seat, and got in. As she pulled out onto the street, she filled him in on the rest—the fake ID, the shell casing, the girl who saw Ashley getting in the van—possibly against her will—the plan to coordinate interviews. As she was finishing up, her phone beeped and she looked at the screen.

"That's Suarez calling in. I want to fill him in on the details. We good? You disengaged yet?"

"I'm getting in the car now," he answered, not taking the bait. "I can be there in fifteen minutes."

"I hope you offered her my apologies, whoever she was," Keri said, unable to keep the sarcasm out of her voice.

"She wasn't the kind of girl who needs apologies," Ray replied.

"Why am I not surprised?"

She switched calls without saying goodbye.

*

Fifteen minutes later, Keri and Ray walked the stretch of Main Street where Ashley Penn may or may not have been abducted. There was nothing obviously out of the ordinary. The dog park next to the street was alive with happy yips and owners shouting out to pets with names like Hoover, Speck, Conrad, and Delilah.

Rich bohemian dog owners. Ah, Venice.

Keri tried to force the extraneous thoughts out of her head and focus. There didn't seem to be much to go on. Ray clearly felt the same way.

"Is it possible she just took off or ran away?' he mused.

"I'm not ruling it out," Keri replied. "She's definitely not the innocent little princess her mom thinks she is."

"They never are."

"Whatever happened to her, it's possible she played a role in it. The more we can get into her life, the more we'll know. We need to talk to some people who won't give us the official line. Like that senator—I don't know what's going on with him. But he definitely wasn't comfortable with me probing into their life."

"Got any idea why?"

"Not yet, other than a gut feeling that there's something he's hiding. I've never met a parent so blasé about their missing child. He was telling stories about pounding beers at fifteen. He was trying too hard."

Ray winced visibly.

"I'm glad you didn't call him on it," he said. "The last thing you need is an enemy who has the word *Senator* in front of his name."

"I don't care."

"Well, you should," he said. "A few words from him to Beecher or Hillman, and you're history."

"I was history five years ago."

"Come on—"

"You know it's true."

"Don't go there," Ray said.

Keri hesitated, glanced at him, then turned her gaze back to the dog park. A few feet from them, a little brown-furred puppy was happily rolling on its back in the dirt.

"Want to know something I never told you?" she asked.

"I'm not sure."

"After, what happened, you know—"

"Evie?"

Keri felt her heart clench at her daughter's name.

"Right. There was a time right after it happened, when I was trying to get pregnant like crazy. It went on for two or three months. Stephen couldn't keep up."

Ray said nothing. She continued.

"Then I woke up one morning and hated myself. I felt like someone who'd lost a dog and went straight to the pound to get a replacement. I felt like a coward, like I was being all about me, instead of keeping the focus where it belonged. I was letting Evie go instead of fighting for her."

"Keri, you got to stop doing this to yourself. You're your own worst enemy, you really are."

"Ray, I can still feel her. She's alive. I don't know where or how, but she is."

He squeezed her hand.

"I know."

"She's thirteen now."

"I know."

They walked the rest of the block in silence. When they got to the intersection at Westminster Avenue, Ray finally spoke.

"Listen," he said in a tone that indicated he was focusing on the case again, "we can follow every lead that turns up. But this is a senator's daughter. And if she didn't just go for some joyride, the claws are going to come out on this one. Sometime soon, the Feds are going to get involved. The brass downtown are going to want in too. By nine tomorrow morning, you and I will be kicked to the curb."

It was probably true but Keri didn't care. She'd deal with the morning in the morning. Right now they had a case to work.

She sighed deeply and closed her eyes. After partnering with her for a year, Ray had finally learned not to interrupt her when she was trying to get in the zone.

After about thirty seconds she opened her eyes and looked around. After a moment, she pointed to a business across the intersection.

"Over there," she said and started walking.

This stretch of Venice north of Washington Boulevard up to about Rose Avenue was a weird crossroads of humanity. There were the mansions of the Venice Canals to the south, the fancy shops of Abbot Kinney Boulevard directly east, the commercial sector to the north, and the grungy surf and skate section along the beach.

But throughout the entire area were gangs. They were more prominent at night, especially closer to the coast. But LAPD Pacific Division was tracking fourteen active gangs in greater Venice, at least five of which considered the spot Keri was standing on as part of their territory. There was one black gang, two Hispanic ones, a white power motorcycle gang, and a gang comprised primarily of drug- and gun-dealing surfers. All of them existed uneasily on the same streets as millennial bar-goers, hookers, wide-eyed tourists, homeless vets, and long-time granola-chomping, tie-dyed T-shirt–wearing residents.

As a result, business in the area comprised everything from hipster speakeasies to henna tattoo parlors to medicinal marijuana dispensaries to the place Keri stood in front of now, a bail bondsman's office.

It was on the second story of a recently restored building, just above a pressed juice bar.

"Check it out," she said. Above the front door, the sign read Briggs Bail Bonds.

"What about it?" Ray said.

"Look right above the sign, above 'Bail.'"

Ray did, confused at first, then squinted his one good eye to see a very small security camera. He looked in the direction the camera was pointing. It was trained on the intersection. Beyond that was the stretch of Main Street near the dog park, where Ashley had allegedly entered the van.

"Good catch," he said.

Keri stepped back and studied the area. It was probably busier now than it had been a few hours ago. But this wasn't exactly a quiet area.

"If you were going to abduct someone, is this where you'd do it?"

Ray shook his head.

"Me? No, I'm more of an alley guy."

"So what kind of person is so brazen as to snatch someone in broad daylight near a busy intersection?"

"Let's find out," Ray said, heading for the door.

They walked up the narrow stairwell to the second floor. The Briggs Bail Bonds door was propped open. Immediately inside that door to the right, a large man with an even larger gut was settled into a recliner, perusing *Guns & Ammo* magazine.

He looked up when Keri and Ray walked in, made the snap decision that they weren't a threat, and nodded to the back of the room. A long-haired man with a scruffy beard sitting at a desk waved them over. Keri and Ray sat in the chairs in front of the man's desk and waited patiently as he worked the phone with a client. The issue wasn't the ten percent cash down, it was the collateral for the full amount. He needed a deed of trust on a house, or possession of a car with a clean title, something like that.

Keri could hear the person on the other end of the line pleading but the long-haired guy wasn't moved.

Thirty seconds later he hung up and focused on the two people in front of him.

"Stu Briggs," he said, "what can I do for you, Detectives?"

Nobody had flashed a badge. Keri was impressed.

Before they could answer he looked more closely at Ray, then nearly shouted.

"Ray Sands—The Sandman! I actually saw your last fight, the one with the southpaw; what was his name?"

"Lenny Jack."

"Right, right, yeah, that's it, Lenny Jack—the Jack Attack. He was missing a finger or something, wasn't he? A pinky?"

"That was after."

"Yeah, well, pinky or not, I thought you had him, I really did. I mean, his legs were rubber, his face was a bloody pulp. He was tripping all over himself. One more good punch, that's all you needed; just one more. Hell, a half-punch would have been enough. You probably could have just blown on him and he would have fallen over."

"That's what I thought too," Ray admitted. "In hindsight, that's probably why I let my guard down. Apparently he had one punch left he wasn't telling anyone about."

The man shrugged.

"Apparently. I lost money on that fight." He seemed to realize that his loss wasn't as great as Ray's and added, "I mean, not that much. Not compared to you. It's not that bad, though, the eye. I can tell it's fake because I know the story. I don't think most people could though."

There was a long silence as he caught his breath and Ray let him twist awkwardly. Stu tried again.

"So you're a cop now? Why exactly is the Sandman sitting in front of my desk with this pretty little lady, excuse me, pretty little peace officer?"

Keri didn't appreciate the condescension but let it slide. They had bigger priorities.

"We need to look at your security camera footage from today," Ray said. "Specifically from two forty-five to four PM."

"Not a problem," Stu answered as if he got this kind of request every day.

The security camera was operational, necessary, actually, given the establishment's clientele; it wasn't just live-time to a monitor but streamed to a hard drive where it was recorded. The lens was wide angled and picked up the entire intersection of Main and Westminster. The video quality was exceptional.

In a back room, Keri and Ray watched the footage on a desktop monitor. The section of Main Street in front of the dog park was visible to about halfway up the block. They could only hope that whatever happened took place on that stretch of road.

Nothing eventful happened until about 3:05. School had obviously just let out as kids began streaming across the street, headed in all directions.

At 3:08, Ashley came into view. Ray didn't recognize her immediately so Keri pointed her out—a confident-looking girl in a skirt and tight top.

Then, just like that, there it was, the black van. It pulled up next to her. The windows were heavily tinted, illegally so. The driver's face wasn't visible as he wore a cap with the brim pulled low. Both sun visors were down and the glare from the bright afternoon sunlight made getting a clear view of the interior of the vehicle impossible.

Ashley stopped walking and looked in the van. The driver seemed to be speaking. She said something and moved closer. As she did, the vehicle's passenger door swung open. Ashley continued to speak, appearing to lean in toward the van. She was engaged in a conversation with whoever was driving. Then, suddenly, she was inside. It wasn't clear if she got in voluntarily or was pulled in. After a few more seconds, the van casually pulled out into the street. No peeling out. No speeding. Nothing out of the ordinary.

They watched the scene again at regular speed, and then a third time, in slow motion.

At the end Ray shrugged and said, "I don't know. I still can't tell. She ended up inside, that's all I can say for certain. Whether it was against her will or not, I'm not sure."

Keri couldn't disagree. The clip was maddeningly indeterminate. But something about it wasn't right. She just couldn't put her finger on it. She rewound the footage and let it replay to the point when the van was nearest the security camera. Then she hit pause. It was the only moment when the van was completely in shadow. It was still impossible to see inside the vehicle. But something else *was* visible.

"You seeing what I'm seeing?" she asked.

Ray nodded.

"The license plate is covered," he noted. "I'd put that in the 'suspicious' category."

"Same here."

Suddenly Keri's phone rang. It was Mia Penn. She dove right in without even saying hello.

"I just got a call from Ashley's friend Thelma. She says she thinks she just got pocket-dialed from Ashley's phone. She heard a bunch of shouting like someone was yelling at someone else. There was loud music playing so she couldn't tell exactly who was doing the shouting but she thinks it was Denton Rivers."

"Ashley's boyfriend?"

"Yes. I called Denton on his phone to see if he'd heard from Ashley yet, not letting on that I'd just talked to Thelma. He said he hadn't seen or heard from Ashley since school but he sounded squirrelly. And this Drake song, "Summer Sixteen," was playing in the background when I called. I called Thelma back to see if that was the song she heard when she got butt-dialed. She said it was. So I called you right away, Detective. Denton Rivers has my baby girl's phone and I think he might have her as well."

"Okay, Mia. This is really helpful. You did a great job. But I need you to stay calm. When we hang up, text me Denton's address. And remember, this could all be completely innocent."

She hung up and looked at Ray. His one good eye suggested he was thinking the same thing she was. Within seconds, her phone buzzed. She forwarded the address to Ray as they hurried down the stairs.

"We need to hurry," she said as they ran to their cars. "This is *not* innocent at all."

CHAPTER FOUR

Keri braced herself as, ten minutes later, she drove past Denton Rivers' home. She slowed her car, examining it, and then parked a block away, Ray behind her. She felt that tingling in her stomach she got when something bad was about to happen.

What if Ashley is in that house? What if he's done something to her?

Denton's street was littered with a series of cookie-cutter one-story houses, all way too close together. There were no trees on the street and the grass on most of the tiny front lawns had long since turned brown. Denton and Ashley clearly did not share similar lifestyles. This part of town, south of Venice Boulevard and a few miles inland, did not have any million-dollar homes.

She and Ray walked quickly together down the block, and she checked her watch: just after six. The sun was beginning its long, slow descent over the ocean to the west, but it wouldn't be truly dark for another couple of hours.

When they reached Denton's house, they heard loud music coming from inside. Keri didn't recognize it.

She and Ray approached in silence, now hearing shouting—angry and serious, a male's voice. Ray unholstered his weapon and motioned for her to go around back, then signaled the number "1," as in they would enter the house in exactly one minute. She looked down at her watch to confirm the time, nodded, took out her own gun, and scurried along the edge of the house toward the back, making sure to duck when she passed open windows.

Ray was the senior detective and he was usually the more cautious between them when it came to entering private property. But he clearly thought these were exigent circumstances that didn't require a warrant. They had a missing girl, a potential suspect inside, and angry shouting. It was defensible.

Keri checked the side gate. It was unlocked. She opened it as little as possible to avoid squeaking and squeezed through. It was unlikely anyone inside could hear her but she didn't want to take any chances.

Once in the backyard, she hugged the rear wall of the house, keeping her eyes open for movement. A ratty, decrepit shed near the property's back fence made her uneasy. The rusty corrugated door looked like it was about to fall off.

She crawled up on the back patio and held there for a moment, listening for Ashley's voice. She didn't hear it.

The rear of the house had an unlocked wooden screen door, which led to a 1970s-style kitchen with a yellow fridge. Keri could see someone down the hall in the living room, shouting along with the music and flailing his body as if he were head-banging in some kind of invisible mosh pit.

There was still no sign of Ashley.

Keri looked down at her watch—any second now.

Right on time, she heard a loud knock on the front door. She opened the rear screen door in tandem with the sound, masking the slight click of the door latch. She waited—a second loud knock let her close the rear door concurrently. She moved swiftly through the kitchen and down the hall, glancing in every open doorway as she went.

Back at the front door, which was open except for the screen, Ray knocked hard, then even harder. Suddenly Denton Rivers stopped dancing and moved to the door. Keri, hiding at the edge of the living room, could see his face in the mirror beside the door.

He looked visibly confused. He was a good-looking kid—short-cropped brown hair, deep blue eyes, a wiry, sinewy frame that suggested he was more likely a wrestler than a football player. Under normal circumstances he was probably a catch, but right now those good looks were masked by an ugly grimace, bloodshot eyes, and a gash on his temple.

When he opened the door, Ray flashed his badge.

"Ray Sands, Los Angeles Police Department Missing Persons Unit," he said in a low, firm voice. "I'd like to come in and ask you a few questions about Ashley Penn."

Panic spread across the kid's face. Keri had seen that look before—he was about to run.

"You're not in trouble," Ray said, sensing the same thing. "I just want to talk."

Keri noticed something black in the kid's right hand, but because his body partially blocked her view, she couldn't tell what it was. She raised her weapon, training it on Denton's back. Slowly, she unlocked the safety.

Ray saw her do it out of the corner of his eye and glanced down at Denton's hand. He had a better view of the item the kid was holding and hadn't raised his own gun yet.

"Is that the remote for the music, Denton?"

"Uh-huh."

"Can you please drop it on the ground in front of you?"

The kid hesitated and then said, "Okay." He dropped the device. It was indeed a remote.

Ray holstered his weapon and Keri did the same. As Ray opened the door, Denton Rivers turned around and was startled to find Keri standing in front of him.

"Who're you?" he demanded.

"Detective Keri Locke. I work with him," she said, nodding at Ray. "Nice place you got here, Denton."

Inside, the house was trashed. Lamps were smashed against walls. Furniture was pushed over. A bottle of whiskey sat on an end table, half empty, next to the source of the music—a Bluetooth speaker. Keri turned the music off. With the room suddenly quiet, she took in the scene more meticulously.

There was blood on the carpet. Keri made a mental note but said nothing.

Denton had deep scratches on his right forearm that could have come from fingernails. The gash on the side of his temple was no longer bleeding but had been at some point recently. The torn shreds of a picture of him and Ashley lay scattered on the floor.

"Where are your parents?"

"My mom's at work."

"What about your dad?"

"He's busy being dead."

Keri, unimpressed, said, "Welcome to the club. We're looking for Ashley Penn."

"Screw her."

"Do you know where she is?"

"No, and I don't give a rat's ass. Me and her are done."

"Is she here?"

"Do you see her?"

"Is her phone here?" Keri pressed.

"No."

"Is that her phone in your back pocket?"

The kid hesitated and then said, "No. I think you should leave now."

Ray got uncomfortably close to the kid, held out his hand, and said, "Let me see that phone."

The kid swallowed hard, then fished it out of his pocket and handed it over. The cover was pink and looked expensive.

Ray asked, "This is Ashley's?"

The kid stood silent, defiant.

27

"I can dial her number and we can see if it rings," he said. "Or you can give me a straight answer."

"Yeah, it's hers. So what?"

"Sit your ass on that couch and don't move," Ray said. Then to Keri, "Do your thing."

Keri searched the house. There were three small bedrooms, a tiny bathroom, and a linen closet, all innocuous looking. There were no signs of struggle or captivity. She found the pull line for the attic in the hallway and tugged. Down came a set of creaky, wooden suspension steps leading upstairs. She carefully climbed up. When she got to the top, she took out her flashlight and pointed it around. It was more of a bonus crawl space than a real attic. The ceiling was only about four feet high and cross beams made it difficult to move around, even while crouching.

There wasn't much up there. Just a decade's worth of spider webs, a bunch of dust-covered boxes, and a bulky-looking wooden trunk at the far end.

Why did someone put the heaviest, creepiest item at the far end of the attic? It had to be hard to get it all the way to that corner.

Keri sighed. Of course someone would put it there just to make her life difficult.

"Everything okay up there?" Ray called out from the living room.

"Yup. Just checking out the attic."

She climbed up the last stair and squatted her way across the attic, making sure to step on the narrow wooden beams. She worried that a wrong step would send her crashing through the drywall ceiling. Sweaty and covered in dusty spider webs, she finally reached the trunk. When she opened it and shined the flashlight inside, she was relieved to discover there was no body. Empty.

Keri closed the trunk and made her way back to the stairs.

Back in the living room, Denton hadn't moved from the couch. Ray was sitting directly front of him, straddling a kitchen chair. When she walked in, he looked up and asked, "Anything?"

She shook her head. "Do we know where Ashley is yet, Detective Sands?"

"Not yet, but we're working on it. Right, Mr. Rivers?"

Denton pretended not to hear the question.

"Can I see Ashley's phone?" Keri asked.

Ray handed it to her unenthusiastically. "It's locked. We'll have to get tech to work their magic."

Keri looked at Rivers and said, "What's her password, Denton?"

28

The kid scoffed at her. "I don't know."

Keri's dour expression let him know she wasn't buying it. "I'm going to repeat the question again, very politely. What's her password?"

The kid hesitated, deciding, and then said, "Honey."

To Ray, Keri said, "There's a shed out back. I'm going to go check it out."

Rivers' eyes darted quickly in that direction but he said nothing.

Out back, Keri used a rusty shovel to pry a padlock off the shed. A strip of sunlight pierced the interior through a hole in the roof. Ashley wasn't in there, just paint cans, old tools, and other random junk. She was just about to step back outside when she noticed a stack of California license plates on a wooden shelf. On closer examination, there were six pairs, all with stickers for the current year.

What are these doing here? We'll have to have them bagged.

She turned around and started to leave when a sudden breeze slammed the rusty door closed, blocking out most of the light in the shed. Thrust into semi-darkness, Keri felt claustrophobic.

She took a huge gulp of air, then another. She tried to regulate her breathing when the door creaked open, letting some sunlight back in.

This must have been what it was like for Evie. Alone, thrust into darkness, confused. Is this what my little girl had to face? Was this her living nightmare?

Keri choked back a sob. She'd pictured Evie locked away in a place like this a hundred times. Next week it would be five years exactly since she disappeared. That was going to be a tough day to get through.

A lot had happened since then—the struggle to keep her marriage together as their hopes faded, the inevitable divorce from Stephen, going on "sabbatical" from her professorship in criminology and psychology at Loyola Marymount University, officially to do independent research but really because the drinking and sleeping around with students had forced the administration's hand. Everywhere she turned, she saw the broken pieces of her life. She'd been forced to face her ultimate failure: the inability to find the daughter who'd been stolen from her.

Keri roughly wiped the tears from her eyes and chastised herself silently.

Okay, you've failed your daughter. Don't fail Ashley too. Get it together, Keri!

Right there in the shed, she powered up Ashley's phone and typed in "Honey." The password worked. At least Denton was honest about one thing.

She tapped *Photos*. There were hundreds of pictures, most of them standard fare—adorable little selfies of Ashley with friends at school, she and Denton Rivers together, a few photos of Mia. But scattered throughout, she was surprised to see, were other, edgier pictures.

Several were taken in an empty bar or club of some sort, clearly before or after hours, with both Ashley and her friends visibly drunk and in hardcore party mode, shotgunning beers, lifting their skirts and flashing their thongs. In some they were working bongs or rolling joints. Bottles of liquor were rampant.

Who did Ashley know that had access to a place like that? When was it happening? When Stafford was in DC? How did her mother have no clue about any of it?

It was the photos with the gun that really caught Keri's attention. It would suddenly be there in the background, a 9mm SIG, sitting inconspicuously on a table next to a pack of cigarettes, or on a couch next to a bag of chips. In one instance, Ashley was out in the woods somewhere, down by a river, shooting at Coke cans.

Why? Was it just for fun? Was she learning how to protect herself? If that was it, then from what?

Interestingly, the photos with Denton Rivers tapered off considerably over the last three months, corresponding with new ones of a strikingly good-looking guy with a long, wild mane of thick blond hair. In many of the pictures, he was shirtless, showing off his six-pack abs. He seemed very proud of them. One thing was certain—he was definitely no high school kid. He looked closer to his early twenties.

Was he the one who had access to the bar?

Ashley had also taken a number of erotic photos of herself. In some, she was flashing her panties. In others she was naked except for a thong, often touching herself suggestively. The photos never showed her face but they were definitely Ashley. Keri recognized her room. In one she could see the bookcase in the background with the old math book hiding her fake ID. In another she could see Ashley's stuffed animal in the background, resting on her pillow with its head turned away, almost as if it couldn't bear to watch. Keri felt the urge to throw up but forced it down.

She went back to the phone's main menu and tapped on *Messages* to see the girl's texts. The erotic pictures from *Photos* had been sent one by one from Ashley to someone named Walker, apparently the guy with the six-pack. The accompanying messages left little to the imagination. Despite Mia Penn's special connection with her daughter, it was starting to look like Stafford Penn understood Ashley much better than her mom did.

There was also a text to Walker four days ago that said, *Formally kicked Denton to the curb today. Expecting drama. I'll let you know.*

Keri powered the phone off and sat there in the dark of the shed, thinking. She closed her eyes and let her mind wander. A scene formed in her head, one so real that she might as well have been right there.

It was a nice, sunny September Sunday morning, filled with endless blue California skies. They were at the playground, she and Evie. Stephen was returning that afternoon from a hiking trip in Joshua Tree. Evie wore a purple tank top, white shorts, lacy white socks, and tennis shoes.

Her smile was wide. Her eyes were green. Her hair was blond and wavy, pulled into pigtails. Her upper front tooth was chipped; it was a grown-up tooth, not a baby one, and would need to be fixed at some point. But every time Keri brought it up, Evie went into full panic mode, so it hadn't happened yet.

Keri sat on the grass, barefoot, with papers scattered all around her. She was getting ready for her keynote speech tomorrow morning at the California Criminology Conference. She'd even lined up a guest speaker, an LAPD detective named Raymond Sands whom she'd consulted with on a few cases.

"Mommy, let's get frozen yogurt!"

Keri checked her watch.

She was almost done and there was a Menchie's on the way home. "Give me five minutes."

"That means yes?"

She smiled.

"It means big, big yes."

"Can I get sprinkles or just fruit toppings?"

"Let me put it like this—how do you spread fairy dust?"

"How?"

"You *sprinkle* it! Get it?"

"Of course I get it, Mommy. I'm not *little*!"

"Of course you're not. My apologies. Just give me five minutes."

She returned her attention to the speech. After a minute, someone walked past her, briefly casting the page in shadow. Annoyed by the distraction, she tried to regain her concentration.

Suddenly, the quiet was shattered by a bloodcurdling scream. Keri looked up, startled. A man in a windbreaker and baseball cap was running away quickly. She could only see the back of him but could tell he was holding something in his arms.

Keri got to her feet, looking desperately around for Evie. She was nowhere to be found. Keri started running after the man even before she knew for sure. A second later, Evie's head poked out from in front of the man. She looked terrified.

"Mommy!" she screamed. "Mommy!"

Keri chased after them, breaking into a full sprint. The man had a big head start. By the time Keri was halfway across the grassy field, he was already in the parking lot.

"Evie! Let her go! Stop! Someone stop that man! He has my daughter!"

People looked around but they mostly seemed confused. No one got up to help. And she didn't see anyone in the parking lot to stop him. She saw where he was headed. There was a white van at the far end of the lot, parallel parked near the curb for an easy exit. He was less than fifty feet from it when she heard Evie's voice again.

"Please, Mommy, help me!" she pleaded.

"I'm coming, baby!"

Keri ran even harder, her vision blurry with burning tears, pushing past the fatigue and fear. She had reached the edge of the parking lot. The asphalt was crumbly and dug into her bare feet as she ran but she didn't care.

"That man has my daughter!" she screamed again, pointing in their direction.

A teenage kid in a T-shirt and his girlfriend got out of their car, only a few spots from the van. The man ran right by them. They looked bewildered until Keri yelled again.

"Stop him!"

The teenager started to walk toward the man, then broke into a run. By then the man had reached the van. He slid the side door open and tossed Evie in like a sack of potatoes. Keri heard the thump as her body slammed against the wall.

He slammed the door shut and started to run around to the driver's side when the teenage boy reached him and grabbed his shoulder. The man spun around and Keri got her best look at him. He was wearing sunglasses and a cap pulled low and it was hard to see through the tears. But she caught a glimpse of blond hair and what looked like part of a tattoo on the right side of his neck.

But before she could discern anything else, the man reared his arm back and punched the teenager in the face, sending him crashing into a nearby car. Keri heard a sickening crack. She saw the man pull a knife from a sheath attached to his belt and plunge it into the teenager's chest. He pulled it out and waited a second to watch the kid tumble to the ground before hurrying around to the driver's seat.

Keri forced what she'd just seen out of her head and focused on nothing but reaching that van. She heard the engine start and saw the van start to pull out. She was less than twenty feet away.

But the vehicle was picking up speed now. Keri kept running but she could feel her body start to give out. She looked at the license plate, ready to commit it to memory. There was none.

She reached for her keys, then realized they were in her purse, back on the field. She ran back to where the teenager was, hoping to grab his and take that car. But when she got to him, she saw his girlfriend kneeling over him, sobbing uncontrollably.

She looked up again. The van was far off in the distance now, leaving a trail of dust. She had no license plate, no description to speak of, nothing to offer the police. Her daughter was gone and she didn't know how to get her back.

Keri dropped to the ground beside the teenage girl and began to weep anew, their wails of despair indistinguishable from each other.

When she opened her eyes she was back in Denton's house. She didn't remember coming out of the shed or walking across the dead grass. But she had somehow gotten to the Rivers' kitchen. This was twice in one day.

It was getting worse.

She walked back into the living room, looked Denton in the eyes, and said, "Where's Ashley?"

"I don't know."

"Why is her phone in your possession?"

"She left it here yesterday."

"Bullshit! She broke up with you four days ago. She wasn't here yesterday."

Denton's face sagged visibly at the verbal gut punch.

"Okay, I took it from her."

"When?"

"This afternoon at school."

"You just snatched it out of her hand?"

"No, I bumped into her after the final bell and snuck it from her purse."

"Who owns a black van?"

"I don't know."

"A friend of yours?"

"No."

"Someone you hired?"

"No."

"How'd you get those scratches on your arm?"

"I don't know."

""How did you get that bump on your head?"

"I don't know."

"Whose blood is that on the carpet?"

"I don't know."

Keri shifted her feet and tried to hold back the fury rising in her blood. She could feel herself losing the battle.

She stared through him and said, without emotion, "I'm going to ask you one more time: where is Ashley Penn?"

"Screw you."

"That's the wrong answer. You think about that on the way down to the station."

She turned away, hesitated briefly, and then suddenly swung back around and punched him with a closed fist, hard, with every ounce of frustration in her body. She got him square in the temple, in the same spot as his previous wound. It split open and blood shot everywhere, some landing on Keri's blouse.

Ray stared at her in disbelief, frozen. Then he jerked Denton Rivers to his feet with one powerful yank and said, "You heard the lady! Move! And don't trip and hit your head on any more coffee tables."

Keri gave him a wry smile for that one but Ray didn't smile back at her. He looked horrified.

Something like this could cost her her job.

She didn't care, though. All she cared about right now was getting this punk to talk.

CHAPTER FIVE

Monday
Evening

Keri drove the Prius with Ray in the passenger seat as they followed the black-and-white she'd called to transport Rivers down to the station. Keri listened quietly as Ray worked the phone.

The captain in charge of the West LA Division was Reena Beecher, but she would be notified of the situation by the head of Pacific Division's Major Crimes Unit, Keri and Ray's boss, Lieutenant Cole Hillman. That's who Ray was filling in now. Hillman, or "Hammer," as some of his underlings called him, had jurisdiction over missing persons, homicide, robbery, and sex crimes.

Keri wasn't a huge fan. To her, Hillman seemed more interested in covering his own ass than putting it on the line to solve cases. Maybe seniority had made him soft. He had no qualms about tearing into detectives who didn't clear their boards—their running tally of open cases. Thus the nickname "Hammer," which he seemed to love. But to Keri's mind he was a hypocrite who got pissed when they didn't close cases *and* got pissed when they took risks to solve those very cases. Keri thought a more appropriate nickname was "asshole." But since she couldn't call him that, her little rebellion was to never call him by his preferred nickname either.

Keri sped through the city streets, trying keep up with the squad car in front of her. Next to her, Ray recapped for Hillman how a late afternoon call about a teen who had been missing for a couple of hours had suddenly morphed into a potentially real abduction situation involving the fifteen-year-old daughter of a US senator. He described the bail bond security video, the visit to Denton Rivers' place (minus some details) and everything in between.

"Detective Locke and I are bringing Rivers down to the station for more questioning."

"Hold on, hold on," Hillman said. "What's Keri Locke doing on this case? This is way above her pay grade, Sands."

"She caught the call, Lieutenant. And she's uncovered almost every lead we have so far. We're almost to the station. We'll fill you more then, sir."

"Fine. I'll be in soon myself. I have to call Captain Beecher anyway. She's going to want a heads-up on this. I've ordered an all-hands in fifteen. "

He hung up without another word.

Ray turned to Keri and said, "We'll get kicked to the curb as soon as they get a full debriefing out of us, but at least we made some progress."

Keri frowned.

"They're going to screw it up," she said.

"You're not the only good investigator in this town, Keri."

"I know. There's you too."

"Thanks for the mildly condescending compliment, partner."

"You bet," she replied, then added, "Hillman doesn't like me."

"I don't know about that. I think he just finds you a little...brash for someone with so little experience."

"That could be it. Or he could just be an asshole. That's okay. I don't like him either."

"Why do you say that?"

"Because he's a toady and a paper pusher and can't think outside the box. Also, when he passes me in the hall, his eyes don't go above my chest."

"Oh. Well, if you're going to hold that against every cop who does that, you'll be left with nothing but assholes."

Keri looked over at him knowingly.

"Exactly," she said.

"I'll try not to take that personally," he said.

"Don't be so sensitive, Iron Giant.'

He sat quietly for a moment in the passenger seat. Keri could tell he wanted to say something but wasn't sure how to bring it up. Finally he spoke.

"Are we going to talk about what happened back there?"

"What?"

"You know, you assaulting an underage boy."

"Oh, that. I'd rather not. Besides, I thought you said he hit his head on the coffee table."

"If it turns out he's not involved in this and he files a complaint, there could be consequences."

"I'm not worried."

"Well, I am. Maybe it's because we're getting close to the anniversary. Have you called Dr. Blanc lately?"

Keri's silence gave him his answer.

"Maybe you should," he said softly.

Keri pulled into the Division parking lot, effectively ending the conversation.

Denton Rivers was put in an interrogation room while Keri filled out the charging complaint against him for theft of property, specifically Ashley's cell phone. It would be enough to hold him for a few hours. By then, with any luck, they'd know more.

After that, they headed to Conference A, the big room where watch commanders doled out assignments at the start of shift. Hillman's all-hands meeting was about to start.

When they arrived, Hillman and six of the Division's most seasoned detectives were already waiting, including two from homicide. Ray fit right in. Keri wasn't as confident. Right now, with all their eyes trained on her, she felt like a bug under a magnifying glass.

Don't sabotage yourself. You belong here, too.

Lt. Cole Hillman stood up to speak. He had recently turned fifty but the deep creases in his face hinted at a man who'd been prematurely aged by the things he'd seen on the job. His salt and pepper hair had begun to recede only slightly. He had a barrel chest and a slight paunch that he tried to hide with loose-fitting shirts. It was after seven in the evening but he still wore a jacket and tie. Keri couldn't remember ever seeing him without them.

"First of all, thank you all for coming in on such short notice. As many of you already know, this case involves Ashley Penn, the daughter of US Senator Stafford Penn. Even if he wasn't close friends with the mayor and the governor, this would be a high priority. But he is, so the pressure is really on. We can expect assistance from our friends at the Bureau shortly. But for now, we need to proceed as if this will remain our case. My understanding is that the senator isn't confident that this was an abduction. He thinks his daughter may be off partying somewhere. That's possible. The video footage of her getting in that van is inconclusive. But until his suspicions are borne out, we will run every lead to ground, understand?"

Heads nodded and there was a general murmur of understanding from the assembled. Hillman continued.

"Apparently, word has spread among the students at the girl's school, West Venice High, and this thing is already starting to blow up on social media. We've already received the first call from a local reporter poking around. By morning, it'll likely be the lead story on every news outlet in the state. So let me be clear—when the media approaches you, and they will, you have no comment. No matter who's asking the question, you refer them to the public information officer. Is that understood?"

Everyone nodded.

"Okay, good," Hillman said. "Right now, we probably have just a few hours to work this before the Feds formally claim jurisdiction. Let's make them count."

With that, he tuned to Ray and said, "Detective Sands, would you please bring us all up to speed."

Ray, leaning against a wall in the back of the room, shifted uncomfortably and said, "If it's all the same, sir, Detective Locke broke this case and knows a lot more about it than I do. I think she's better prepared."

Everyone looked at Keri, who was standing next to her partner.

Hillman scowled but said, "Detective Locke, it looks like the floor is yours."

Her chest tightened. A vision of a white van tearing down a road as her bloody feet burned flashed before her eyes for the briefest of moments.

"Detective Locke? Are you okay?" Hillman asked.

Ray nudged her.

"Keri—" he whispered.

"Yes sir, just gathering my thoughts," she said, snapping to. She thought about moving to the front of the room but decided against it. She liked having the wall to lean on for support.

It only took a moment for her nervousness to subside as she got into the details of the case. She walked them through what had occurred so far, largely in chronological order. She showed the surveillance footage of the van, then connected Ashley's phone into a large flat-screen monitor and showed pictures from the *Photos* album.

She held nothing back, even though she knew that once she shared everything, her value to the case would be gone in Hillman's eyes and he could remove her. But if that meant Ashley was found, it was a small price to pay.

"What's the deal with this Rivers kid? Is he a legit suspect?" Detective Manny Suarez asked. He'd been the one Mia Penn had called earlier at Keri's instruction. A squat, sleepy-eyed man in his forties with permanent stubble, Suarez was much sharper than he let on, which was by design.

"Denton Rivers, the ex-boyfriend, is in Interrogation Two. He hasn't been especially cooperative so far. He still needs to be thoroughly questioned to see if he was the one driving the black van, if he hired someone to do it, or whether he knows anything useful. Ashley dumped him four days ago. It's possible he flipped out—thought that if he couldn't have Ashley, no one could. He has motive, but that's not going to be enough to hold him if we don't find more."

Keri took a breath and glanced around the room. Everyone was at rapt attention. It seemed that at least they were taking this seriously. She continued.

"CSU needs to process his house on Woodlawn. They need to test the blood on the carpet to see if it's a match for Ashley. There were also six pairs of apparently stolen license plates in the shed. The owners of those plates need to be questioned about when they went missing and if they saw who took them. Every surveillance camera in the area on Main, Westminster, and the surrounding streets needs to be reviewed as soon as possible. Ashley's new love interest, Walker, needs to be found and questioned. All of Ashley's friends and teachers at school need to be located and questioned."

Detective Suarez piped in at that point.

"I've compiled a list based on what Mia Penn told me on the phone. We can start to reach out as soon as the meeting's over."

"Thanks, Manny. We may need to pull in someone from the drug task force too. Ashley was clearly getting pot from someone. Her dealer should be found and questioned. I have a feeling he'll know more about the other side of Ashley's life, things her friends might be reluctant to reveal. Same thing for whomever it was that made the fake ID for her."

In the front of the room, Lt. Hillman took a short call from someone and then waved for Keri to stop talking.

He switched the monitor to TV mode and flicked to the news. Local anchor Amber Smith, an LA institution, had interrupted tonight's episode of *Jeopardy!* with a breaking news update.

"We are getting reports that Ashley Penn, the daughter of California Senator Stafford Penn, is missing. She reportedly vanished after leaving West Venice High School this afternoon."

A photo of Ashley appeared on the screen along with a phone number. Amber continued.

"This is a very preliminary report and has not been verified as of this time, but anyone knowing anything about the whereabouts of Ashley Penn should call the Los Angeles Police Department at the number on your screen. We will update this story as news develops and have a full report on Action News at eleven. Now back to your regularly scheduled programming."

Hillman turned off the monitor. He looked frustrated but not surprised.

"That's our cue, folks. We're going to divide everything up and get going. Also be clear; this is a team effort. I'm going to repeat that. This is a team effort. If you're thinking of jockeying for position or withholding information for your own advantage or doing anything that doesn't move this case along as fast as possible, I want you to stand up now and walk out of this room."

Everyone looked around. No one stood up.

"Okay, then, let's get moving. Brody, you supervise the search at Rivers' house on Woodlawn. Edgerton, work with tech to see if we can get any quality location tagging off that phone. Suarez, get Ashley's friends, Thelma Gray and Miranda Sanchez, in here for interviews. Make sure they each have a parent with them. We don't need any blowback. Patterson, coordinate with all the local businesses near the school to get any security footage they have. You're on the black van hunt. Sterling and Cantwell, you've got the Denton Rivers questioning. He's in Interrogation Two."

Everyone scrambled out of the conference room.

Keri and Ray were left alone in the room with Hillman, unsure what to do. They hadn't been given assignments. Hillman pointed at them.

"You two come with me."

CHAPTER SIX

Monday
Evening

Hillman led them into his small office. There was a comfy-looking couch against the wall but he directed them to the two uncomfortable metal chairs in front of his desk and sat down across from them. Keri could barely see him over piles of files that took up most of his desk.

"Good work out there, Detectives. Ray, you know that Brody's retiring at the end of the year, right?"

"Yes, sir."

"That means there will be an opening in Homicide. You interested?"

Keri watched Ray's mouth drop open. He stared at Hillman, then at her. She smiled at him even as her heart sank. That seemed to help him regain his composure.

"Do I have to answer right now?"

"Of course not. Just don't wait too long. There's a lot of interest but I want you to apply for it."

Thank you, sir."

Hillman nodded, then turned his attention to Keri.

"Locke, first off, well done. It was your tenacity that got this case rolling. We'd really be behind the eight ball if you hadn't gotten that head start. And after that rough beginning, you nailed the breakdown in the all-hands meeting in there. I think you've got a real future here."

She felt it coming.

"But…" she said.

Hillman looked genuinely pained.

"*But* this case is getting political fast. We have to tread lightly considering who's involved. And we're probably only hours from the Feds taking over. We can't have any missteps."

"There won't be," she promised.

Hillman's eyes flashed. Any sympathy he'd had disappeared from his face.

"Denton Rivers threatened to file a complaint against you for assault."

"For what?" Keri demanded, displaying more self-righteousness than she felt.

"How about that massive welt on his head?"

41

"He already had that when we got there. And then he tripped and hit it on a coffee table."

"Stow that bullshit! Don't insult my intelligence, Detective. The decision has been made. We can't have any more suspects tripping into coffee tables. You're off the case."

"Off?" she repeated, stunned.

Hillman nodded.

"We'll still tap you as a resource if need be. You're obviously well versed in the case particulars. But beyond that, yes, you're off. I can't risk anything that puts a conviction in jeopardy."

Ray cleared his throat.

"With all due respect, sir—"

Hillman held up his hand.

"Don't waste your breath, Sands. The decision has been made."

He continued to talk but Keri didn't hear it. An image flashed through her head of a little girl being tossed into a van, of a loud thud as her body slammed into the wall. Then a voice snapped her out of it.

"Locke, are you there?"

Hillman's voice was loud, as if he'd asked the question more than once.

She said, "Yes, sir."

"Okay. That's it then. Go home and get some sleep."

Ray stood up and said, "Sir, if she's off the case, I'm off too."

Lieutenant Hillman frowned.

"I need you to coordinate the surveillance footage with Patterson."

Ray exhaled, deciding, then said, "Detective Locke is my partner. We're both on or we're both off."

The look on Hillman's face was one Keri had never seen before. His mouth twisted into a warped pucker. The lines in his forehead formed even deeper grooves than usual. He seemed to be desperately struggling to contain his temper.

"It wasn't a request, Detective Sands," he finally growled.

"In that case, sir, I'm not feeling very well. I think I need to take some sick time."

Keri said softly, "Ray, don't."

He ignored her, staring hard at Hillman with his one good eye.

The older man stared back, and after what felt like an eternity, seemed to relent. He shook his head in disbelief and said, "Fine. Take your 'sick time.' Now get out of here before I suspend you."

They walked out of his office.

Keri turned to him; he looked as dazed as she felt.

42

"What do we do now?" Keri asked.

"Meet me at your car in five minutes. I have to wrap a few things up."

"Where are we going?"

"To get drunk," he answered.

*

Fifteen minutes later, at just after eight, they sat at a tiny corner booth at Clive's, a Culver City bar popular with cops. Keri was on her second Glenlivet. Ray sipped a light beer.

"Trying to keep your girlish figure?" she teased.

"I have to stay in shape in case the next suspect you attack tries to fight back."

"I deserved that. You know, I'm starting to think that having me for a partner isn't all that great for your career, Ray."

"*Starting* to think...?" he asked incredulously.

"Seriously—I don't have much in the way of impulse control and you always to seem to bear the brunt of that. You stood by me with Hillman, so now he's pissed at you, possibly putting that Homicide job at risk. I'm like a human tire fire. You should stay clear of me."

"What if I don't want to stay clear of you?" he asked with more sincerity than Keri was prepared for.

She downed some more scotch and let it warm her insides. The shots were starting to take the edge off and she considered giving a heartfelt response. Was there a better time to address this than now? Her position in the unit was in question. Ray might be moved to Homicide. Maybe they should finally shoot straight about what exactly they were to each other—partners, friends, more?

But before she could reply, Ray seemed to lose his nerve and spoke up quickly.

"I mean, if I lost you as a partner, who would teach me all those dope Krav Maga moves?"

Keri felt the moment passing and decided to let it go—for now.

"Yeah, you'd be lost without me. Otherwise, you'd have to depend on those boxing hooks and jabs and crewcuts."

"Uppercuts," he said softly, smiling.

"Yeah, those."

"You know, that's what I thought Lenny Jack was coming at me with in that last fight, an uppercut. But he surprised me with that hook and—blam—goodbye eyeball. I was too arrogant."

"Arrogant isn't a word that comes to mind when I think of you; cocky, maybe, but not arrogant."

"You didn't know me back then, Keri. I was arrogant. I was raking in pretty good money. I had nice things. I had a woman who loved me and two kids who adored me. And I took it all for granted. I burned through cash like it was going out of style. I cheated on my wife. I didn't spend time with my children. I treated people badly. And I went into that fight lazy, feeling entitled. I got what I deserved."

"Don't say that."

"It's true. I deserved to lose that fight. And I deserved to go bankrupt. I deserved to have Delilah leave me and take the kids. And I deserved to lose that eye too. Looking back, it actually changed my life

for the better. I actually started to give a shit about other people. It gave me the freedom to try to make a difference. It's weird to say, but it may be the best thing that ever happened to me. Well, almost the best thing."

Pretending not to pick up on that last comment, Keri nodded. They'd both had life-changing events which sent them on a new career path. The difference was that for Ray, law enforcement was a calling. For her, it was a mission with one ultimate goal—to find her daughter.

"I had the dream again last night," she said.

"The one at the park?"

She nodded.

"This time I got so close. I was running so fast. I looked down and saw my bare feet leaving bloody footprints in the gravel. I could almost reach out and touch the back of the van. Evie was looking at me through the rear window. She was screaming but no sound came out. The van hit a bump and she dropped out of sight. Then I woke up. I was so soaked in sweat that I had to change clothes."

"I'm sorry, Keri," Ray said. She refused to look up at him, afraid to let him see that her eyes were damp.

"Ray, am I ever going to find her?"

"We'll find her together. I promise. And when we do, she'll have a lot of birthday parties to make up. Maybe I'll come as a clown," he added, trying to lighten the mood. She decided to go along.

"Because that's not scary at all."

"What do you mean? I'm a sweetheart!"

"You're a pituitary case. Putting you in clown makeup isn't going to make it better, Paul Bunyan."

"Whatever you say, Fievel."

Keri opened her mouth to fire back when Ray's phone rang. He answered it before she could get a word out.

"Saved by the bell," she muttered.

"What's up?" he asked the person on the other end of the line. He listened, pulling out his notepad and writing furiously. He didn't say a word until the very end.

"Thanks, Garrett. I owe you."

"What is it?" Keri asked after he'd hung up.

"We gotta go," he said, standing up and dropping some bills on the table. They headed for the door.

"Who was that?"

"Detective Patterson. Before we left the station I asked him to call me with any major updates. He's been checking surveillance from near the school. You know how the front license plate on the van was covered up?"

"Yeah?"

"Well, it looks like the guy forgot to cover the rear one. The security camera from a tattoo parlor on Windward caught it. They got a hit. It belongs to a guy named Johnnie Cotton. He's got a long rap sheet. I can fill you in on the details in the car. But the most important one is that he's a small-time drug dealer."

"Why does that matter?"

"Because you know one of his clients."

"Who's that?" Keri asked as they hurried down the street to her car.

"Denton Rivers. Patterson said the kid just admitted it to Sterling and Cantwell. That's who gave him the first bump on his head and the scratches too. Apparently Denton hadn't been paying his bills."

"You're thinking that Johnnie Cotton took Ashley as collateral?"

"It's a theory."

"So why are we in such a hurry?"

"First give me your keys," Ray said.

"Why?"

"Because you don't handle your Glenlivet as well as you think you do."

Keri had to admit that the warm feeling from the shots hadn't subsided. She tossed him her keys.

"Now will you tell me why we're in such a rush?"

45

"Because Patterson told me that Hillman's assembling a strike team to hit Cotton's place. They'll be there in about forty-five minutes."

"So what?"

"So, Cotton lives near the Baldwin Hills oil fields."

"That's ten minutes from here," Keri said.

"Yes, it is. Care to go on a field trip?"

"I thought we were off the case."

"You're off the case. I'm on sick leave. But I'm feeling better all of a sudden. Can I help it if you were in the car with me when I decided to pursue a viable lead?" He was grinning from ear to ear.

"Hillman's going to kill you."

"Not if he wants me to take that Homicide job, he's not. So are you in or not?"

Keri raised her eyebrows.

Did this guy forget who he's talking to?

"Drive," she said.

Within seconds they were tearing down the street, siren blaring. If they made good time, they'd be at Cotton's place a half hour before the cavalry.

And if Ashley's hurt, you're going to be begging for them to show up.

CHAPTER SEVEN

Monday
Night

As they weaved through the late rush hour traffic, Ray reviewed the info Patterson had given him on Johnnie Cotton. He'd been swept up in a child pornography sting six years ago, when he was twenty-four, and ended up spending two years in Lompoc. Out now, he would be on the sex offender registry for the rest of his life. That might explain why he lived in an industrial section of town, where it was far less likely that he'd violate the rule to stay 100 feet away from any schools or playgrounds.

But as troubling as that offense was, it wasn't what had them headed to his place now. Instead, it was his van and Denton's allegation that he was his dealer. Those two things together were enough for Hillman to get a warrant for his strike force. But Lieutenant Cole Hillman was a cautious man. Keri and Ray were both confident that just like the yelling they heard at Denton's house, these details about Cotton created exigent circumstances that didn't require a warrant. Neither of them needed to say it out loud: they were going in.

Cotton lived adjacent to Baldwin Hills, a wealthy, primarily African-American neighborhood in the heart of West Los Angeles. Most of the homes were on sloping hills that rose high enough to give panoramic views of the city on light smog days. But Cotton didn't live in that neighborhood. His place was just to the south, in a mostly desolate stretch of land populated by oil fields and the always pumping derricks that sucked them dry.

His two-acre property was just off Stocker Street, on a stretch of Santa Fe Road, littered with rock and gravel suppliers, fabrication shops, junk yards, and the ramshackle homes of those businesses' owners.

Keri and Ray got to Cotton's place just after sunset. They had turned off the siren when they pulled off nearby La Cienega Boulevard. Now Ray turned off the headlights as well. They parked on the street, several hundred feet down from Cotton's place, near the adjacent property. It was some sort of graveyard for broken down bulldozers, excavators, and eighteen-wheelers, which cast eerie black silhouettes against the fast darkening sky.

There were no streetlights in the area, exacerbating the shadows. A few of the buildings had small lights over the doorways but they were so far off the road that they weren't much help to Keri and Ray.

They reviewed the plan before going any further.

"We've got about twenty-five minutes, tops, before the strike team arrives," Ray noted. "Let's keep our focus on finding Ashley and getting her out safe. We'll let the pros handle the takedown if possible. Sound good?"

Keri nodded.

The side gate for the vehicle graveyard property parallel to Cotton's place was open so they entered as quietly as possible.

I guess the owner of this place isn't too concerned about anyone making off with his stuff unnoticed.

The properties were only divided by a five-foot-high chain-link fence. They carefully traversed the area for a hundred yards, before they finally saw a structure on Cotton's property. It was a small one-story house with yellow interior lights peeking through the pulled curtains.

Behind it, farther back into the blackness, they could now see several other structures, the largest of which looked like a two-story metal building—possibly a welding shop from the look of it—followed by several others, smaller and more shed-like. None of them had any interior or exterior lighting.

They climbed over the fence, landed on Cotton's property, and approached the house quietly, moving in a wide searching circle, navigating through the broken husks of old rusty cars squatting on flat, airless tires.

Except for the dull hum of traffic a half mile away and the distant barking of one lonely dog, they heard nothing.

"I don't see a van," Keri whispered. She tried to ignore the sweat creeping down her back, making her shirt cling to her clammy skin. Despite the sweltering heat, she felt a chill.

"He might not be home."

They kept moving, one careful step at a time, never quite sure if they were about to snag a tripwire or step on a homemade explosive of some sort. With a guy like Johnnie Cotton, who clearly didn't like unannounced visitors, you could never tell.

They got all the way to the house and peeked through the narrow gap between the curtains. They could see a small living room. An old tube TV with rabbit-ears sat in one corner with nothing but static on the screen. There didn't seem to be any movement inside. The light they'd seen came from a table lamp. A small fan on the floor oscillated back and forth in a futile attempt to keep the place cool. Other than the hum of the blades, they heard no sound coming from inside.

They crept around the side of the house, passing a blacked out and closed window, and then continued to the back, where a sliding window was in the up position for air flow. Through the screen, they saw a bedroom. A bit of light trickled into the room from a hall, enough to show that the bedroom walls were plastered with magazine pictures of young girls, almost all of whom were in outfits like nighties and bathing suits. It wasn't kiddie porn—everything on the walls was available at a newsstand. But the sheer volume of it was disturbing.

"Old habits die hard, I guess," Ray muttered,

They continued their search, looking in every available window, and finally concluded that the man wasn't home. They found the back door, which Ray unlocked with a credit card, entered, and did a quick search of the place, flicking on light switches only when necessary and only for a few seconds, in case Cotton came back unexpectedly.

In the closet off the main bedroom, Ray spotted a shoebox on an upper shelf. He started pull it down when they both heard a noise below them, sort of a scurrying sound. They froze, staring at each other.

"Ashley?" Ray mouthed silently.

"Or maybe Cotton, hiding," Keri whispered back.

Keri pulled back the area rug in the living room, revealing a trap door. There was a snap lock on it but nothing else to prevent them from opening it. Keri holstered her gun and put her hand on the lock while Ray trained his gun on the door. She silently counted down from three with one hand while bracing herself to open the door with the other. At the end of the count she yanked open the door so that it lay flat on the floor, then stood aside.

For a second there was nothing. Then they heard the scurrying again. As it got closer it sounded more like a gallop. And then something shot out from the basement below, almost faster than the eye could see.

A huge German shepherd landed on the floor on all fours, growling. Its fur was matted and Keri could smell it from halfway across the room. The dog swiveled its head around and caught sight of Ray in the closet. He growled again and bounded in that direction, his clawed paws scraping noisily on the wooden floor.

"Shut the door!" Keri yelled. Ray did as he was told, managing to slam it closed just before the animal reached him. The shepherd turned around immediately, looking for the source of the voice. His eyes locked on Keri. She saw his muscles tense as he prepared to leap.

Unlike Ray, she was in the center of the living room. There was no way she'd make it to a doorway before the dog got to her.

What am I going to do?

She realized her hand was already resting on her holstered gun. She didn't want to use it but feared she wouldn't have much choice. It was clear that the dog had been trained to attack and she doubted he'd go easy on her. Suddenly a voice called out from the closet.

"Hey, ugly! Come and get me!"

The dog turned to glance at the closet door briefly. Keri used the reprieve to glance quickly around the room.

Nowhere to go. He's faster than me. I can't outrun him. I can't outfight him. I don't even know if I can pull my gun before he reaches me.

The dog lost interest in the voice and returned his attention to Keri. Then an idea popped into her head. But to make it work she'd need another distraction. It was if Ray had read her mind. He opened the closet door a crack and shouted again.

"What's the problem, Cujo—scared?"

The shepherd barked and tried to shove his nose through the door, without success.

That was all Keri needed. She knelt down quickly. The dog gave up on Ray and focused on Keri. Ray continued to yell but the animal ignored him. A long strand of saliva hung from his open mouth. His teeth seemed to gleam in the dull lamplight. There was a beat of stillness and then he leapt, a canine torpedo headed straight for her. Out of the corner of her eye, Keri saw Ray open the closet door, his gun pointed at the fast-moving dog.

"No!" Keri shouted as she yanked the trap door upright to create a barrier between her and the dog. The animal, already in the air, could do nothing to avoid it and slammed into the door before falling down the basement stairs. Even as she started to push the door shut, Keri saw the shepherd scrambling back up the stairs, apparently unhurt. She slammed the door closed a fraction of a second before the dog smashed into it. She heard it slip down the stairs again for a second, then gather itself again for another leap.

She lay down on the trap door, pressing all her weight against it, and braced for the next collision. When it came, it knocked her in the air a few inches. By the time she caught her breath, the dog was roaring up the stairs for a third time.

But by now, Ray had reached her and dove on the trapdoor as well. This time, when the dog slammed into it, there was no movement. They heard a loud yelp, then the soft patter of the dog retreating down the stairs, apparently finally defeated.

Keri rolled over, snapped the door locked, and let out a huge sigh. Ray lay next to her, breathing heavily. After a few seconds Keri sat up and looked at him.

"Cujo?" she asked.

"It was all I could think of."

They both slowly got to their feet and looked around. Keri noticed that the shoebox in the closet that Ray had been holding had fallen to the ground, spreading hundreds of photos on the floor. They were all of naked girls ranging in age from five or so to the late teens.

Without even thinking, Keri started tearing through them, looking for Evie, until Ray put his hand on her shoulder and quietly said, "Not now."

"Ray!"

"Not now. That's not what we're here for. Besides, they're not going anywhere. Come on."

She hesitated and then snatched the box from the closet floor and ran with it into the living room, closer to the light of the lamp. There she dumped the remaining pictures on the floor before Ray could stop her and began to rapidly shuffle through them.

Evie's in here. I know it.

Ray tried to grab her wrist but she twisted free.

"She's in here, Ray! Leave me alone!"

"Look!" he hissed, pointing at the driveway.

Suddenly the front of the house lit up.

Headlights were coming at them, still a ways off but approaching fast. It was Cotton, coming home.

"Come on!" Ray insisted.

They got the pictures back in the box and in the closet, straightened out the carpet over the trap door, and somehow managed to step out the back door just as Cotton entered through the front. They stood there, motionless, wondering if he'd heard the door shut. A second passed and then another. The back door didn't open. No head peered out to see if anything was there. Ray tugged softly on Keri's arm and they quietly worked their way through the darkness further back onto the property.

At the two-story structure, a metal prefabricated building, Keri said, "Let's go back."

"No."

"Ray—"

"No, you're going to shoot him."

51

"Only if he gives me a reason."

"He's already given you a reason."

"Ray, come on."

"No, it's for your own good. Remember why we're here—to find Ashley. We're Missing Persons, not vigilantes. Besides, the strike force will be here in a few minutes to take care of him."

Keri nodded silently. He was right. She needed to stay focused now. There was time to review the pictures later. They turned their attention back to the building before them. The front door was unlocked. Inside, it was completely dark.

Keri softly called, "Ashley!"

No response.

"Stay here and cover me," she said. "I'm going to check it out."

"Don't turn on any lights."

"Don't worry. And let me know if Cotton tries to bail."

Ten steps inside, she was totally blind. She pulled out her tiny flashlight and slowly waved it around the room.

"Ashley!"

No one answered.

There's no way this can be a dead-end. She has to be here somewhere.

She checked around corners and behind doors but found nothing. The place was huge and there were too many places to hide—or be stashed away. They needed some real light.

Just as she had the thought, the building was bathed in light. Keri ducked, unsure of what was going on. Ray hid behind a fifty-five-gallon drum near the entrance. Then she realized that headlights had been turned on from a vehicle next to the house. The lights swung around and then disappeared down the long gravel driveway to Santa Fe Road.

Keri sprinted back to Ray but by the time she reached him, he was already on the phone.

"Suspect is driving a black van, headed north on Santa Fe Road."

He paused to listen to the speaker on the other end of the line.

"Copy that. No evidence of missing girl in the house. Unknown whether suspect is armed. We'll remain at the location in case he returns. Sands out."

He turned to face Keri.

"That was Brody. He's with the strike team. He says they've got Cotton under surveillance. Hillman's apparently dealing with some other secret crisis right now but he was conferenced in on our call. He doesn't want to use the strike force until he has to. If Ashley's not anywhere here on the property, he's hoping Cotton will lead them to her location."

Keri started to respond but he interrupted.

"I know what you're thinking. Don't worry. There are six vehicles trailing him and he's driving a big black van. He's not getting away, Keri."

"That's not what I was thinking."

"It's not?"

"Okay, yes, it was. But you don't have to be so condescending about it."

"Sorry."

"I forgive you. Now let's take advantage of the situation."

They headed back to the two-story metal building. Keri felt around for the light switch and flipped it on. The place sprang to life. It was full of fabrication machinery and tools. A quick search revealed that Ashley wasn't there. They found a crowbar and proceeded to pry open every shed on the lot. They searched them all. Every one of them was empty.

They shouted at the top of their lungs.

"Ashley!"

"Ashley!"

"Ashley, are you here?"

She wasn't.

Keri headed back to the house at a fast walk with Ray right behind her. She pushed hard through the back door and went straight to the closet and swung open the closet door.

The shelf was empty.

The shoebox was gone.

Keri hunted around briefly for it before her frustration got the better of her. She grabbed the lamp from the living room end table and threw it against the wall. The ceramic base shattered all over the floor. The dog below the floorboards began to bark. He'd found his courage again.

She slumped down on the couch and hung her head. Ray, who'd been standing quietly by the back door, walked over and sat down next to her.

He was about to speak when Keri's phone buzzed. She picked up. It was Mia Penn.

"Detective Locke, where are you?"

"Looking for your daughter, Mrs. Penn," she answered, trying to hide how deflated she felt.

"Can you come over here right now?"

"Why? What's going on?"

53

"Please, just get here as fast as you can."

CHAPTER EIGHT

The Stafford residence was in chaos. Keri and Ray had to fight their way through a media circus to get in the house. Even inside, they could hear the shouts from reporters. A different security staffer from before led them into a massive kitchen, where they found Mia in tears and Stafford pacing back and forth angrily. When she saw them walk in, Mia wiped her eyes and cleared her throat.

"We had a long visit from a guy who apparently runs everything at Pacific Station," Mia said. "Cole Hillman."

"I guess we know what the secret crisis was," Keri said to Ray. Then to Mia, "Yep, that's our boss."

"Well, he said he had this huge experienced team in place and that he'd personally be leading it and that you did a great job but now you were off the case."

"That's true," Keri said.

"I told him no way," Mia said. "Then he said you didn't have the experience."

Keri nodded. It was true.

"I've only been a detective for a year now."

"When I didn't back down, he also said you weren't ready for the pressures of a case like this, that you had a daughter abducted five years ago and that you never really recovered. He said that sometimes you just drift off for minutes at a time or think that every little girl is your daughter."

Keri exhaled.

Who in the hell did Hillman think he was talking to a civilian like that? Wasn't this some kind of HR violation?

Still, she couldn't deny it.

"Yeah, that's pretty much true also."

"Well, when he said it, he made it sound like a bad thing," Mia said. "But I can tell you something right here and now. If Ashley is still missing in five years, that's exactly what I'll be doing—seeing her face everywhere I look."

"She won't be—"

"Yeah, hopefully, but that's not the point. The point is, you get it—you get what's going on here—and he doesn't have a clue. I told him point-blank that I not only want you back on the case, I want you heading it up. Stafford backed me a hundred percent."

The senator nodded.

"There wouldn't be a case right now if it wasn't for you," he said.

Keri felt her stomach twist in a knot.

"I think you're underestimating Lieutenant Hillman."

"Regardless, Stafford and I want you on the case and we made our opinion clear."

"What did he say?"

"He said it was a complex matter, he's been in law enforcement a long time, and he has a far better understanding of who to bring into the case to get things done than either of us did. He was polite about it, but in the end he basically took the position that a couple of civilians, even one who's a senator, weren't about to tell him how to run his department."

"There's a lot of merit to that."

"Maybe, but I don't care. We want you handling this and we told him so."

Keri considered it and then shook her head.

"Look, I appreciate the vote of confidence, but—"

"But nothing. You're heading it up as far as we're concerned. We're not even going to talk to anyone else."

"What about me?" Ray asked with a smile, trying to lower the tension in the room.

"Who are you?" Mia asked, seemingly noticing him for the first time.

"This is my partner, Ray Sands. He taught me pretty much everything I know about being a cop."

"Then I guess you can stay," Mia replied in what sounded like a slightly lighter tone. "Now, tell us what's new—anything?"

Keri brought them up to date on what happened at Denton Rivers' house, and how they got the license plate of the black van and had just now searched the premises of the van's owner, an ex-con named Johnnie Cotton, only to find Ashley nowhere around. She didn't mention that the guy was their daughter's drug dealer or anything about the surveillance. She didn't want to raise false hopes.

Stafford looked hard at her and said, "If you were in charge, what would you do, right this minute?"

She considered it.

"Well, we're following up a few leads I can't discuss yet. But if they don't pan out in the next hour, I think I'd get an Amber Alert out. That way, a description of both Ashley and the black van would be broadcast throughout the media. Sometimes we hold off on that if we think it would put the child at greater risk. But I don't really see a downside in this situation. Ray?"

"No, if our current leads don't shake out we'd blast out all relevant information and see what came back."

"Including the license plate number?" Senator Penn asked.

"Correct," Ray said. "But as Detective Locke mentioned, we need to see how a couple of leads develop before taking that next step."

"I understand it was you two who found the black van in the first place?" Mia asked.

"Right," Ray answered.

"And not Cole Hillman and his huge, experienced team?"

"Mrs. Penn—" Keri started.

"Mia. I think you can go with the first name under the circumstances."

"Okay, Mia, and please call me Keri. Yes, Ray and I found the van. But Lieutenant Hillman is just doing what he thinks is best. We're all doing everything we can to get your daughter back. Let's try to work together rather than at cross purposes, all right?"

Mia nodded.

"How long does it take to get the Amber Alert out?"

"Once it's approved, only a matter of minutes," Ray told her. "I can get the preliminaries started now so that we can pull the trigger immediately once we get approval."

Mia looked at Stafford for his support.

He hesitated.

"Stafford?"

He had a look of doubt on his face and said, "We've suddenly got all this craziness going on in her life. Lieutenant Hillman mentioned a fake ID, photos showing pot and alcohol and…nudity. He mentioned some new guy who's way older than she is. Part of me still wonders if she just went off to party with some guy in a van and is too wasted to get in touch. If she wanders home in the morning drunk, after an Amber Alert goes out, my career, quite frankly, is over. Hell, considering the press frenzy, it may be over anyway."

Mia pressed his hand.

"She's in serious trouble, Stafford, I can feel it. She won't be wandering in drunk. She needs us now, right this second. She needs everything we can give her. Forget about your career and think about your daughter. If it turns out that she *was* taken and we didn't do this, you'd never forgive yourself."

He exhaled, weighing the options one last time, then looked at Keri and said, "Let's get it going then, if we can."

"Okay," Keri said, "let us track down these last few leads. If nothing materializes, we'll post the alert within the hour. We should head out."

"Can I at least offer you something to eat before you go?" Mia asked. "When's the last time you had a meal?"

Almost immediately upon hearing the question, Keri's stomach began to growl. She'd had nothing since lunch, almost nine hours ago. Plus, the shots she'd had at the bar had given her a dull headache. She glanced at Ray and could tell he was thinking the same thing.

"Maybe some sandwiches, if it's not too much trouble," he said. "It's not like we can do anything else until we hear back from Brody."

"You're not able to tell us what these leads you keep referencing are?" Senator Penn asked.

"Not yet. They could be useful. They could be nothing. We don't want you riding any more of an emotional roller coaster than you already are."

"I hate roller coasters," Mia muttered to no one in particular.

Ten minutes later, as they finished wolfing down their sandwiches, Ray's cell rang.

"Sands here," he said through a full mouth. He listened intently for a minute while everyone else remained silent. When he hung up, he turned to them. Keri could tell it was bad news before he spoke.

"I'm sorry to say our leads didn't pan out. We had a surveillance team following Johnnie Cotton as he drove around town in his van. At some point he made them and they had to take him down. Ashley wasn't in the van. He's down at the station right now."

"Is he being questioned?" Senator Stafford asked.

"He was but he started asking for a lawyer pretty much from the get go. He's been in this kind of situation before. He knows there's no advantage for him in talking."

"Maybe he'd be more receptive if Detective Locke had a conversation with him," Senator Penn suggested.

"Maybe—she's great with interrogations. But I don't think Hillman would go for it. This case has a lot of heat already and I don't think he wants to do anything to jeopardize a conviction."

"Lieutenant Hillman left me his card earlier. I think I will use it. Why don't you two go down to the station? I have a feeling that by the time you get there, he'll have had a change of heart."

"Senator, with all due respect, once a suspect asks for a lawyer, there's a ticking clock. There's only so long you can hold them before it's viewed as a gross violation of rights."

"Then you'd better get down there fast." He stared at them both with such certitude than they couldn't help but wonder if it was possible. Keri looked at Ray, who shrugged.

"Let's go," he said. "No harm in trying."

They headed for the door, escorted once again by the security guard. They were almost outside when Mia ran after them. She opened her mouth but before she could speak, Keri beat her to it.

"Don't worry, Mia. I'll order the Amber Alert as soon as we get in the car. We'll get her back soon."

Mia gave her a small hug, then waved to the security guard to help them navigate the throng of press just beyond the gate. With their shouted questions and bright camera lights, the reporters seemed like jackals now. But very soon, they could be a useful tool to get a teenage girl back home to her family.

So why do I have such a sinking feeling in the pit of my stomach?

CHAPTER NINE

Monday
Night

Johnnie Cotton was already in Interrogation Room 1 when Keri got to the station. She'd dropped Ray off at his car by Denton Rivers' house and expected him to arrive any second. Hillman wasn't around but Detective Cantwell caught her in the hall outside the room and told her that Hillman had put her back on the case and that she was authorized to question Cotton. He said it flatly, without emotion, but beneath that she could sense the veteran detective's disdain. She chose to ignore it.

While she waited for her partner to arrive, she stared at Johnnie Cotton through the one-way mirror of the interrogation room. Since they'd tried to avoid him back at his place, this was her first real chance to get a look at him.

He didn't look like the stereotype of a pedophile. His eyes didn't constantly water. His chin wasn't especially weak. His shoulders didn't slope. He wasn't particularly pudgy or pale. He was just a regular-looking guy—dark hair, medium build, maybe a little pimply-faced for a thirty-year-old man, maybe a little short. But on the whole, he was mostly unremarkable, which was, of course, far more troubling. It would have been preferable if these types were easily identifiable.

He stood in the corner of the room, his hands cuffed in front of him, with his back pressed against the wall. She suspected that had been his default position in prison just to survive. Pedophiles weren't popular there.

Keri made a snap decision. She wasn't going to wait for Ray. There was something about this guy that made her think he'd just shut down if confronted by her partner's looming presence. She'd use it if necessary, but later. She walked into the room.

Cotton's eyes darted at her when she walked in, then twisted away almost immediately.

"Come over here," Keri said. The man complied. "Now follow me."

She led him outside the interrogation room, into the hallway. Cantwell and Sterling, who had been chatting in the hall, turned to them, stunned.

"Locke, what are you doing?" Sterling demanded.

"We'll be right back."

With that, she led him down the hall and into the women's restroom, as her fellow detectives watched with astonishment.

"Wait here," she told them, then closed the door and focused on Cotton.

"There are no cameras in here. There are no microphones in here." She unbuttoned her blouse, exposing her bra and stomach, and said, "I'm not wearing a wire. Whatever you say, it's just between you and me. Tell me you want a lawyer."

The man looked at her, confused.

"Say it," Keri said. "Say, 'I want a lawyer.'"

He complied.

"I want a lawyer."

"No, you can't have one," Keri said. "Do you see what just happened? If this place *was* wired, which it isn't, nothing you say could ever be used against you now because I just denied you your constitutional rights. The bottom line is that we're alone. I'm not here to hurt you. I'm not here to trick you. Do you understand?"

The man nodded.

"The only thing I want is Ashley Penn." The man opened his mouth to speak but Keri interrupted him. "No, no, don't say a word yet. Let me just set the groundwork a little more. Earlier this evening, I broke into your house, looking for Ashley. You weren't home. I saw the shoebox in your closet. I saw all the pictures."

A bead of sweat glistened on the man's forehead.

"When you came home, you saw that they'd been disturbed. Am I right?"

He nodded.

"You knew someone had seen them. You took them somewhere and destroyed them before you were arrested. Am I correct?"

"Yes."

"Well, between you and me, that's not going to work. I saw them and I can testify that I saw them. My testimony will be more than enough to revoke your probation. All I have to do is say the word and you're going straight back to prison. Here's the deal. I get Ashley Penn back and you keep your freedom."

The man paced.

Then he said, "Those photographs, I never wanted them. They just show up in the mail."

"Bullshit."

"No, it's the truth. They just show up."

"From who?"

"I don't know," he said. "There's never a return address on the envelope."

"Well, if you don't want them, why didn't you just burn them?"

He shrugged.

"I couldn't."

"Because you like them too much?"

He exhaled.

"I know it's hard to understand," he said. "I think someone's setting me up. They wanted them in my house. They knew I wouldn't be able to just get rid of them. They wanted the police to find them. They want to send me back to jail. And now here it is, actually happening. I should have burned them all the second they showed up."

"You can still get out of this," Keri said. "Where's Ashley Penn?"

"I don't know."

Keri frowned.

"Tell me what you did with her."

"Nothing."

"I don't believe you, Johnnie."

"Honest to God," he said. "According to the news she got taken after school, right? In the middle of the afternoon?"

"Yes."

"Well, I was at work," he said. "I work down at Rick's Autos in Cerritos. I was there all day. I didn't leave until after five. You can call Rick and he'll tell you. He warned me that if I missed any more time, he'd fire me."

"You miss a lot of time lately?"

"I'll skip a day here and there. But Rick warned me so I was careful to stay the whole day. Besides, they have security cameras there. You can see me in the lot all day long. I never left, not once, not even for five minutes. I even ate my lunch in the break room. Check it out. Call him, he'll tell you."

Keri felt a growing unease. His alibi was so specific that it would be easy to poke holes in it if it wasn't true, which meant it probably was.

"All day?" Keri asked.

"Yeah. At one point, I got a call around two from some dude wanting make a... purchase—"

"Don't worry, Johnnie, I'm not looking to bust you for dealing. Go on."

"Well, he wanted me to meet him in the Cerritos Mall parking lot. But I didn't know the guy and like I said, Rick—"

"Warned you, I know. So if you were there, then who had your van?"

"No one. It was with me all day."

"Someone had it."

"No, no one," he said. "I had it parked right there on the lot. I was literally walking around it all day long. It was right there."

"We have it on videotape taking Ashley."

"That's impossible. It was with me. Go look at Rick's cameras. You'll see."

Keri took Cotton back to the interrogation room. When she stepped out, Ray was waiting for her.

"I can't leave you alone for a second," he said.

"Follow me," she told him, not feeling playful.

They headed to the garage where Cotton's black van was being processed. Keri typed the plate number into the computer. To her astonishment, it didn't match the van. The plates on Johnnie Cotton's van were registered to a white Camry owned by someone named Barbara Green from Silverlake.

"What the hell's going on?" Ray asked, equally stunned.

"You want my theory?" Keri said.

"Please."

"Whoever took Ashley Penn was trying to frame Johnnie Cotton," she said. "He used a black van for the abduction, same make and model as Cotton's. He stole Cotton's plates so that we'd be able to ID him eventually but covered the front one so it would look like Cotton was being sneaky."

Ray joined in.

"And he replaced Cotton's plates with Barbara Green's so the guy likely wouldn't notice the difference until it was too late."

"Exactly," Keri agreed. "And I'm willing to bet that whoever did all that also sent Cotton those pictures of the little girls. Cotton claimed they just showed up in the mail, no return address. Whoever it was knew the guy wouldn't be able to toss them and that we'd find them when we searched the house, making him look even guiltier."

"So Cotton's not our man," Ray said.

"No. But that's not the worst of it. Whoever our guy is has been planning this for a while. He knew Cotton was Denton Rivers' dealer. He knew he was a pedophile. And he actively tried to undermine Cotton's alibi by trying to get him to meet at the mall."

"So we're right back to square one," Ray said.

Keri shook her head.

"Worse than square one," she said. "We've wasted the one thing Ashley Penn doesn't have: time."

63

CHAPTER TEN

Monday
Night

Ashley was having trouble opening her eyes. She knew she was conscious but everything felt heavy and fuzzy. It reminded her of when she was eleven and tore a ligament in her ankle while surfing; she had to have surgery and they'd put her under. When she woke up, she'd had this same feeling, as if she were waking not just from sleep but almost from death.

How long had she been lying there?

Her head already hurt. There was no individual source of the pain. It throbbed all over, so much so that she feared the act of moving would make it worse.

Despite her anxiety about the pain it might cause, Ashley decided it was time to open her eyes.

It was pitch-black. She could see nothing.

And that's when the fear started to hit her. This wasn't a hospital.

Where am I?

She imagined it was what one might feel after being roofied. That set off another spasm of fear.

How did I get to this place? Why can't I remember anything?

She tried to control the terror she felt starting to grip her. She reminded herself of how she handled it when a really huge wave knocked her off her surfboard and forced her down toward the ocean floor. Freaking out did her no good. She couldn't outfight a wave. She had to stay calm and wait it out. She had to feel the fear but let it pass through her so she could take action when the wave passed.

She forced herself to do the same here. She couldn't see and she couldn't remember, but that didn't mean she was helpless. She decided to try to sit up.

She pushed up on her elbows until she was sitting upright, ignoring the jackhammer in her head. After it subsided slightly, she checked herself in the darkness. She was still wearing her top and skirt. Her bra and panties weren't missing but her shoes were. She was on a thin mattress, her bare feet resting on the scratchy wooden floor. Other than the general aching and headache she didn't think she had any injuries.

Her right ear felt funny. She reached up and realized that her earring was missing and her lobe was throbbing. Her left earring was still there.

She reached out to get some sense of her surroundings. The floor was definitely wood but there was something weird about it she couldn't place. She continued to feel around until her fingers bumped into a wall at the head of the mattress. To her surprise, it was metal. She rapped her knuckle on it. Even though it was thick, the noise echoed throughout.

She used the wall to brace herself as she stood up and ran her fingers along it, taking tiny, careful steps. After a moment it became clear that the wall was curved. She followed it around in a circle until her feet bumped into the mattress again. She was in some kind of cylindrical room. It was hard to gauge the size of it but she guessed it was about as big as a two-car garage.

She sat back down on the mattress and was surprised by the sound it made. She stomped her foot on the wooden flooring and realized what had seemed odd about it before: it felt hollow below, like she was on a patio deck.

Ashley sat quietly for a minute, trying to force a memory, any memory, to return to her throbbing head. She could feel the fear beginning to take hold again.

What is this place? How did I get here? Why can't I remember anything?

"Hello!"

A quick echo spit back at her, suggesting a closed structure with a tall ceiling. No one answered.

"Is anybody there?"

Not a sound came.

Her thoughts turned to her parents. Were they looking for her? Had she been gone long enough to make them worry? Would her dad even notice she was gone?

Tears came to her eyes. She angrily wiped them away with the back of her hand. Senator Stafford Penn didn't like crybabies.

"Mom!" she yelled, hearing the panic rise in her voice. "Mom, help me!"

Her throat felt like sandpaper. How long had it been since she drank anything? How long had she been here?

She crawled around on the floor, feeling for anything other than the mattress. To her surprise, her hand bumped into a plastic bin in the center of the room. She got the top off and felt around inside. There were several plastic bottles, various containers, and…a flashlight?

Yes!

Ashley turned it on and the room sprang to life. Almost immediately, she realized it wasn't actually a room. She was in some kind of silo, up near the top where the ceiling funneled to a point ten feet above her head. In the plastic bin were bottles of water, some soup, peanut butter, jerky, toilet paper, and a loaf of bread. Next to the bin was a plastic bucket. She could guess what that was for.

She shined the light along the walls, hoping against hope there might be a door. Nothing. What got her attention, though, was all the writing on the walls.

She moved toward the nearest one, written in black magic marker.

I'm Brenda Walker. I died here July 2016. Tell my mother and father and my sister Hanna that I will always love them.

A phone number followed. It had an 818 area code—the San Fernando Valley.

Jesus!

Ashley moved the light along the walls. There were other messages in different handwriting. Some were short and to the point like Brenda's. Others were long and rambling, seemingly written over a period of days. There were at least a dozen different names, and their messages literally covered the walls.

Ashley felt herself starting to hyperventilate. Her knees wobbled and she dropped to the floor, grabbing the edges of the bin to steady herself. The flashlight fell on top of the loaf of bread. She closed her eyes tight and breathed slowly in and out, trying to force the messages on the wall out of her head.

After a minute she opened her eyes again and glanced back at the bin. The flashlight had rolled off the bread and was lying on the bottom, next to some peanut butter.

A lot of good that will do me, considering I'm allergic to the stuff.

She picked up the flashlight and gave the container of peanut butter a useless whack. As it shifted position in the bin, she saw something underneath it that she'd missed before. She leaned in, looking more closely. It was a thick black permanent magic marker.

And that's when Ashley began to scream.

CHAPTER ELEVEN

Monday
Night

Keri waited at the front door, trying to maintain her patience. She'd been standing here for over two minutes.

After the Johnnie Cotton lead had turned up nothing, Hillman told them to start from scratch. They still had to run down everything Cotton had said for confirmation. Patterson was supervising the CSU search of Cotton's van, just in case something turned up. Sterling was headed to Rick's Autos in Cerritos to meet up with Cotton's boss to review his surveillance video and confirm his alibi.

Edgerton, the tech expert, had taken the cell phone Cotton had happily given him to try to trace the phone of the mysterious caller who wanted to meet up for a drug sale in the mall parking lot. An officer was also bringing him Ashley's home laptop so he could do a deep scan to discover anything she might be hiding.

Suarez was typing up the reports from his interviews with Thelma Gray and Miranda Sanchez. Cantwell was doing a search of sales of black vans matching the abductor's in LA County over the last month and checking the owners for criminal records.

Ray had gone back to Ashley's high school to meet with the principal and review surveillance footage of the surrounding streets in recent days. They hoped the abductor had cased the school and made some kind of mistake, maybe gotten sloppy and gotten out of the van so he could be identified.

Brody had been pulled from the search entirely to investigate a drive-by shooting in Westchester. Hillman himself was reviewing recent cases of teen abductions in the county, looking for similarities.

Keri got Hillman to let her check out Walker Lee, the older guy Ashley seemed to have taken up with in recent weeks. She knew he'd said yes just to get her out of the station and away from the heart of the investigation. But she didn't mind. She didn't have much hope for any of those other areas of pursuit and figured she may as well try a fresh lead.

Walker Lee lived in North Venice just off Rose Avenue. The area was teeming with art galleries, vegan brunch spots, organic spas, and hundreds of artist lofts, which was just a fancy way of describing unfurnished, bare bones studio apartments. But because they were called "lofts" and were located in Venice, the building owners could charge $2,500 a month for 500 square feet. The same place in Sherman Oaks would go for under $1,000.

Lee's place appeared to be a variation on the theme. It was in what looked like an old auto body shop, in which each repair station had been walled off from the others and transformed into a living space. Keri doubted the loud music his neighbors heard coming from his unit was in any way diminished by the cheap drywall separators.

She banged on the front door again. Minutes earlier, Walker Lee had shouted that he'd just gotten out of the shower and needed a minute to get dressed.

"It's been long enough, Mr. Lee. Open up now or I'm going to open this door for you."

A second later, the door opened.

Walker Lee—Ashley's new boyfriend—stood in front of her. He looked like the guy in the photos. As in many of them, he was currently wearing no shirt or shoes, only a pair of jeans with an open button and a half-zipped fly that showcased his six-pack abs. His long blond hair was damp and water dripped from a few strands onto the concrete floor at his feet. He was so beautiful that it took effort for Keri not to stare.

"Come on in. You said you had some questions about Ashley?" he said as he rubbed a towel through his hair.

Keri nodded and followed him into the loft, trying not to stare at his backside. No wonder Ashley had been smitten. This guy was eye candy even by Hollywood standards. He led her through the main area, which served as the bedroom, through the kitchen that used to be a body shop office, and into what she guessed had once been the break room. Keri noticed that the door and walls were padded. Her internal alert system went off briefly as she wondered why he was guiding her into a soundproof room. But when she looked inside, she understood. It had been converted into a tiny rehearsal studio, complete with speaker towers, drums, microphones, soundboards, amplifiers, guitars, boxes, crates, endless wires, and even a couch to crash on. There was barely room to move. Lee plopped down on the couch and waited for Keri to speak. She took a seat in a metal folding chair across from him.

"As I said before, the reason I'm here is Ashley Penn. Do you know where she is?"

The man raked his fingers through his hair, a confused look on his face.

"Home?"

"No."

"She's not here if that's what you're getting at."

"Do you own a black van?"

"No."

"Do you know anyone who owns a black van? Someone in the band, maybe?"

"No. I don't get it. Do you want to tell me what's going on?"

"You don't watch the news?"

"I don't have a TV and since we weren't gigging tonight, I've been rehearsing in here all evening. I only quit to shower fifteen minutes ago."

"Were you alone? Can any of your band mates verify your whereabouts?"

"No. I like to work on new material by myself. Are you asking if I have an alibi? Seriously, what is going on?"

Keri explained how Ashley went missing after school this afternoon, all the while studying his face, trying to detect if he already knew what she was talking about. He betrayed nothing suspicious, only shock. She didn't know if it was genuine or if his performance skills extended to police interviews.

As she spoke he grabbed two shot glasses, splashed whiskey into both, and handed one to Keri.

She shook her head so he set it on a speaker.

"Thanks, but no."

"You don't drink?"

"Not when I'm on duty," she lied. "Who'd want to take Ashley?"

Walker drained his glass.

"There's some stuff going down," he said. "But man, I can't be talking to the cops about it."

"Why not?"

"Because it could all come back to bite me in the ass."

"Look, nothing personal but I don't give a rat's ass about your ass," Keri said. "Unless you had something do with it, I'm not interested in you. So drop the drama and just talk to me."

"Ah, man—"

"You want to help her, right?"

"Of course I do."

"Then talk. Tell me what you know."

He seemed to be contemplating his options, then looked Keri straight in the eyes and said, "Drink your glass first."

"I told you—"

"Yeah, I know, *you're on duty*," he said. "You want me to talk and tell you stuff that might come back to bite me? Fine, then let's even the score. You do something that can come back to bite you. You drink, I talk. That's the deal."

Keri sized him up. Then she picked up the shot glass and leaned in toward him, putting on some of the flirty airs she remembered from a previous lifetime.

"Let me ask you a question first," Keri said, already aware of the answer, "you're how old?"

"Twenty-three. Is that too young for you, Detective?"

"You'd be surprised," she told him, leaning back again. "And Ashley's fifteen, if I recall. So what you've been doing to her is technically statutory rape. I assume that's one of the things you're worried about getting bit by."

The man nodded. Keri put the shot glass back down and stared at him hard.

"Let's be clear, Walker. You don't mind if I call you Walker, do you?"

He shook his head, unsure whether she was still flirting or not. She cleared it up for him.

"Walker, in addition to statutory rape, I'm guessing your phone has a number of nude photos of Ashley. That's possession of child pornography, which is also a sex crime. In fact, each photo is a separate count. Ordinarily I'd call my very large partner and let him punch you until your internal organs oozed out in your stool, but right now I don't have time. The only thing I have time for is finding Ashley. So talk. Tell me something, tell me anything, and stop worrying about yourself for ten seconds. If you're straight with me, you won't have anything to worry about. If you're not, I'm going to be your worst nightmare, I guarantee it."

Walker gulped. It was nice to see the smirk disappear from his face, if only briefly. After he regained his composure, he spilled everything.

According to him, even though his band, Rave, was doing decently here in LA—they even had a single in rotation on KROQ—he didn't think they could break out of the pack. There was just too much competition here. Walker—the lead singer and songwriter—was thinking of dumping the band and going to Vegas to try to make it solo. He was the face of the band, he wrote the songs, he played lead guitar. He figured he'd be a big fish in a smaller pond in the desert. Once he established himself, he could come back and fill theatres instead of clubs. Ashley was going to come with him.

"So you two were going to run away?"

Walker shrugged. "Start living is more like it. I'm going to be huge. She is too. You've seen her, right? She's gorgeous. She'd been looking into some modeling agencies there. They were interested."

His information fit with the web searches Keri had found on the laptop in Ashley's room.

"There was just one little wrinkle," he continued. "She's always had money—never had to ask for it. She knew her parents wouldn't give her any if she just took off. So she started to joke about faking her own abduction and ransoming them."

Keri tried to hide the shock she felt. Could Ashley actually be behind her own disappearance? That didn't fit with anything about the case so far.

"Do you think that's what happened?"

He shook his head.

"No, it was just a joke. If I had to lay money down, I'd put all this crap at the feet of Artie North."

Keri had never heard the name before.

"Who's Artie North?"

"He's a super creepy security guard at Ashley's school. He caught me and Ashley one day, out behind the bleachers, you know, being …affectionate. He got video of it on his phone. Then the little freak tried to bribe Ashley into having sex with him. Otherwise he said he'd upload it to a bunch of porn sites."

"So did she? Have sex with him?"

"No. Someone beat the shit out of him instead."

"You?"

He shrugged.

"I can't recall. The important thing is, she told me he's been giving her dirty looks ever since."

Keri turned it over in her head, trying to make sense of everything she'd been told. Predatory rock star boy toys, creepy security guards, possible faked abductions—she'd just gone from no leads to too many. She stood up.

"Don't leave town, Walker. I'm going to check out every one of these leads. And if it turns out you've been lying to me, I'm going to bring my partner back for an up close and personal visit, you understand?"

He nodded. She grabbed the shot off the speaker, downed it in one swallow, and tossed him the empty glass as she walked out the door.

"And for Christ's sake, put on a frickin' shirt."

Outside, she called Suarez and asked him to work up anything he had on Artie North and get back to her right away. Then she called Ray.

"Where are you?" she asked.

"I just wrapped up at the school. I'm headed back to the station."

"I'll meet you there and pick you up. Don't even go inside."

"What's up?'

"We've got a new suspect. And I'd like your company when I have a little chat with him."

"Okay. You sound peppy."

"I got multiple new leads while getting hit on by a himbo, so you know, confidence boost."

"I'm so happy for you," Ray said sarcastically.

"I knew you would be. See you in five."

Keri hung up, put the siren on her roof, and turned it on. She loved driving with the siren on.

CHAPTER TWELVE

Monday
Night

Keri and Ray pulled into the parking lot for the Lawndale Division 22 Metrolink maintenance and storage yard. Artie North, it turned out, wasn't just a security guard at Ashley's school, but also worked a second job as a security guard at the yard housed just off Aviation Boulevard near Rosecrans Avenue.

Keri didn't love the look of the place. Even in the day, it would have been unsettling. But at night, with limited light, the sprawling yard, full of motionless, hulking metrocars, was downright creepy. It was the sort of place she imagined Evie being held when her nightmares got the better of her.

Suarez had called her back on the drive south and let her know that Artie North owned a van, but it was white, not black. Obviously that didn't clear him, as painting the thing would have been easy.

And what's the deal with all the vans? Is every abduction suspect required to have one?

They walked up to the entrance. There was a large automatic gate in front with a security office off to the right. Keri noticed there was no van in the main lot but she couldn't see the employee lot on the other side of the gate because of the office. No one was visible through the window so Keri pushed the buzzer by the door. Her hand went involuntarily to check her holster. Ray saw her do it and frowned slightly.

"Let's not shoot anyone until we have to, okay. All we have on this guy is the word of your new boy band boyfriend."

"And the van—don't forget the van, Megatron."

Before Ray could respond, a pudgy, sleepy-looking guy walked in from the back room of the office. It appeared they woke him up. Keri didn't like to make snap judgments, but looking at him, she didn't know how he could secure a waist belt, much less a school or a municipal rail yard.

As he walked toward them, Artie North's whole body jiggled. His uniform shirt spilled over his front, seemingly propelling him forward. His face was pale and pimply and his pale blue eyes watered under the fluorescent lights. He looked to be about five foot eight but was well over 250 pounds.

It wasn't hard to imagine that a guy who looked like this spent most of his time watching porn by the dull light of a computer monitor and might have to blackmail compromised teens to get any live action.

As he got close to the window, Keri held up her badge.

"LAPD. Are you Artie North?"

"Yes."

"We'd like to ask you a few questions. May we come in?"

Artie hesitated.

"I should probably call the site manager."

"Mr. North, I wasn't really asking. I was just being polite. You need to open the door."

He did so without another word. As they stepped inside, Ray picked up the questioning.

"You also work security at West Venice High?"

"Uh-huh."

"Are you familiar with a student named Ashley Penn?"

"Sure. She's a sophomore. Why, is something wrong?"

"She's gone missing," Keri said. "You haven't heard?"

"No, I haven't."

That seemed dubious. It had been all over the news. Once they sent out the Amber Alert, the press had been in a permanent frenzy.

Once they were inside, Artie locked the door again and turned back to them.

"Please have a seat."

Keri glanced around. Inside was a first-class security center with radios, landlines, all the equipment a guard could want, and a locked gun case. The back section of the building held sleeping quarters, a small kitchen, and a bathroom.

"What happened to Ashley?" Artie asked.

Keri answered his question with a question.

"Mr. North, how is it that you've heard nothing about this? It's been all over the media."

Artie smiled ruefully as he spread his arm out to showcase the room.

"All this fancy equipment but they don't allow me a TV. And they monitor web use on the computer so I just leave it on the company website. A guy got fired a few months ago for checking out ESPN dot com while on duty."

"Is that hard for you Mr. North, not being able to surf the web for such long stretches?" Keri asked.

He looked at her quizzically.

"What?"

"Never mind. Let me get right to the point. We've received a report that you have a compromising video of Ashley; that you were threatening to release it publicly if she didn't have sex with you."

Artie looked genuinely shocked.

"Absolutely not," he said.

"That's not true?"

"No. Who said such a thing?"

"That's confidential. Do you ever talk to Ashley at school?"

"A little. I talk to everyone."

"What do you say to her?"

"Hi, have a nice day, get to class, typical stuff."

Ray got up and started walking around, as if he were curious about the security equipment. As Artie's eyes followed him, Keri stifled a smile. This was a standard Raymond Sands maneuver to make a person of interest a little less comfortable—wander, loiter, hover. Having a large African-American cop making himself comfortable in their personal space tended to throw most people off their game. Sometimes they let things slip.

"You're working two jobs?" Keri asked, forcing Artie's attention back to her.

"Yes. I work at the school until three and then come here to the yard. I'm on active duty until ten and then go to sleep but I'm here all night if they need me."

"Then you go directly to school in the morning?"

"Yes."

"What days?"

"Monday to Friday. On the weekends I go home."

"Which is where?"

"I have an old farm up near Piru, west of Santa Clarita. It's not really a farm anymore but the property is pretty valuable so I try to keep it in decent shape. Why?"

"When were you there last?"

"This morning, when I left to go to the school. I won't be back there until Friday night, after my shift here ends at ten."

"Do you have a van?"

"Yes."

"Can we see it?"

"Sure. It's at the side of the building."

They took a look. It was still white and very dirty. Ray went over and scratched at the side with his fingertip. It hadn't been washed in weeks and Keri doubted it had been painted since it left the plant where it was assembled. She turned back to Artie.

"Does the rail yard here have any vehicles?"

75

"Sure—"

"Are any of them vans?"

"No, no vans. They're pickup trucks, mostly, and a couple of old SUVs."

Keri switched topics. She could tell that bouncing around was keeping Artie uncomfortable, which was good.

"Ashley's been hanging out with a guy with long blond hair," she said. "He's the singer in a group called Rave. Have you ever seen Ashley with him?"

The man nodded.

"Oh, yeah," he said.

"Where?"

"He'd hang around out past the bleachers where some of the equipment sheds are," he said. "Ashley would go there and meet him after school sometimes."

"To have sex?"

"And sometimes more," he added.

"Meaning what?"

"Well, I got suspicious that they were dealing drugs or something, so I started keeping an eye on them. A couple of months ago I snuck up on them. They had actually broken into one of the sheds. When I looked in, they were, you know, having intercourse."

"Did you take video of it?"

Artie looked horrified.

"No. I told the guy to get the hell off school grounds. He got this real angry look on his face, like he was trying to scare me or something, but I didn't back down. I told him to leave, now, and never come back. He looked like he wanted to punch me but he didn't try. Good thing for him because I was ready for it. In the end he just left. Ashley went with him. The next day she begged me not to tell anyone what I'd seen. I told her I wouldn't as long as her boyfriend stayed off campus."

"When was this?"

"Early last week."

"Did he ever come back?"

"Not that I know of."

"What about any of that made you think they were dealing drugs?" Ray asked, reminding him why he'd started the story in the first place.

"Oh yeah. After they left the shed that day, I noticed some vials on the floor, like four of them. It seemed like too much for just personal use."

"Could you tell what it was?"

"They were all white powder. Could've been coke, heroin, maybe meth. I'm no expert."

"Did you turn it in?"

"Are you kidding? That girl's father is a United States senator. What if she said it wasn't hers and I'm left with all these drugs in my possession? Who are people going to believe? Who's got more power? I tossed the vials in the trash and moved on."

*

Five minutes later, back in the car, Keri drove silently back to the station, lost in thought. Ray finally broke the silence.

"It seems that the stories from Artie North and your boyfriend are a tad contradictory."

"You think?"

"Who do you believe?"

"Do I have to pick? Maybe they're both lying. All I know is my brain is fried. Every lead we get ends up leading us back to the beginning. And if she was taken, she's running out of time."

"Are you starting to doubt that?"

"Ray, I don't know what to believe anymore."

Suddenly her phone rang. She put it on speaker and an unfamiliar female voice said, "Keri Locke?"

"Yes."

"My name's Britton Boudiette. I'm a friend of Ashley Penn's. I'd like to meet with you right away if that's possible."

"What about?"

"About some stuff I'd rather not get into over the phone. Please. It might be important. Don't bring anyone with you. Just you."

Keri took down her info and hung up. Then she turned to Ray and said in a cynical tone she didn't even know she was capable of, "Don't bring anyone with you? In the history of law enforcement, has anything good ever resulted from that sentence?"

CHAPTER THIRTEEN

Twenty minutes later, after dropping Ray back at the station, Keri pulled up in the alley behind Britton Boudiette's house, flashed the high beams three times like she'd been asked, and then killed the lights and the engine.

Almost immediately, a female figure came out from a back bedroom of the house onto a second-story deck. She worked her way down the structure to the ground level, hurried over to the car, and quietly got in the passenger side.

Keri felt ridiculous. She was having a secret meeting in her car with a fifteen-year-old girl in the middle of the night. If the kid's parents found out, she wondered if they could press some kind of charge against her. She put the thought out of her mind and tried to take Britton seriously.

The girl was African-American, pretty, and athletic—currently dressed in flannel cartoon pajama bottoms and a pink T-shirt. She got right to the point.

"Ashley would kill me if she knew I was meeting with you. You absolutely, positively have to keep this on the down low. You can't tell anybody that I ever talked to you."

"I won't, unless absolutely necessary," Keri assured her, essentially promising nothing. Britton seemed satisfied anyway.

"Okay," she said. "I honestly don't know if any of this is going to help anything. Ashley's been sort of crazy lately."

"How so?"

"She has this new boyfriend, Walker Lee, who's the lead singer of Rave, which you probably never heard of but is a very cool band who just released their first single, "Honey." It's pretty awesome. Anyway, Walker's been a terrible influence on Ashley."

"In what way?"

"Well, it started with him getting a fake ID for Ashley, so she could come to the clubs and watch the band. Then there was drugs and drinking, not a lot, nothing crazy, but, you know, Ashley's only fifteen."

"Britton, you're not telling me anything I don't already know," even though Walker being the source of the fake license was news to her.

Britton seemed to waver for a moment, then went on.

"Then they started committing thrill crimes."

"What do you mean?"

"Nothing malicious or violent, just stuff for the adrenaline high, you know? Two weeks ago, they stole a car and went joyriding. They've been having a lot of sex in public places where they could get caught. And last week—do you know where the Nakatomi Plaza is on Avenue of the Stars?"

"Yes."

Keri knew it well.

It was actually called Fox Plaza but it was often referenced as Nakatomi Plaza because that's what it was called in the movie *Die Hard*, at least before it blew up. The thirty-five-story skyscraper was located in the heart of Century City, a west-side enclave known for law firms and talent agencies.

"They hid out in the building until it closed," the girl said. "Then they spent the night up at the top, drinking wine and smoking pot. The next morning they snuck out. Ashley's parents thought Ashley was sleeping over at my house that night. I covered for her but between you and me, I didn't like doing it."

All this was interesting but if it was getting Keri anywhere, she couldn't see it.

"Here's the worst part though," the girl said. "Walker recently bought a gun."

"Why?"

"He's in some kind of trouble. I think someone's after him, and maybe him plus Ashley, I'm not sure. She said it had something to do with Walker losing some drugs he owed to someone. That's the main thing I wanted to tell you. She might be mixed up in something. I don't know. I do know that they were planning on running away to Vegas."

"To become stars of the music and fashion worlds, right?"

"I don't think so. I think it's more to escape whatever it is that's going on here." The girl exhaled. "Ashley's parents don't know any of this and you have to promise not to tell them. I'm only telling you because something in all this may be behind why she disappeared."

Keri patted the girl's arm.

"You're doing the right thing."

"Does any of it help?"

"I don't know yet. Maybe—"

"There's one more thing that you should know," the girl said. "This is something that you absolutely have to promise to not repeat because Ashley told it to me in the strictest secrecy."

"I understand," Keri said, again making no promises.

The girl studied Keri for a moment and then said, "Ashley's mom, Mia, comes from a lot of money. Her parents—meaning Ashley's grandparents—used a law firm here in LA for all their legal work, Peterson and Love. Do you know it?"

Keri nodded. It was one of the largest law firms in the city, very political, with several branches in other states. It had been around forever.

"Yes."

"Okay, well, they used their pull to get their daughter, Mia, a job at the law firm when she was fourteen, in the summer, between ninth and tenth grade. She did photocopying, ran errands, shelved books, and stuff like that."

"Okay."

"Well, Stafford was a partner in that firm at the time," the girl said. "He was thirty that summer. Anyway, he got Mia in his office one night after everyone left and he deflowered her."

"Deflowered?"

"Yeah, that means she was a virgin at the time," Britton said earnestly.

"Oh, right." Keri tried to keep a straight face.

"Don't get me wrong, it was consensual, but he was a full-grown man, a lawyer no less, and Mia was just a kid. She got pregnant. He wanted her to get an abortion but she refused and ended up having the child—Ashley. After that, Mia and Ashley moved to Paris for seven years and then came back here. Mia was twenty-two when they came back and Ashley was seven."

"This is…I don't know…wild," Keri said.

"Trust me, I know," the girl said. "Mia and Stafford struck things up again after that long gap and eventually they got married and he formally 'adopted' Ashley. He never technically denied being her birth father but by adopting her, most people just assumed he was her stepdad. Anyway, it was Mia's idea for Stafford to get into politics and she funded his campaigns. That's how he became a senator. No one outside their inner circle knows that he is actually the blood father. If the public ever found out how their family was created, his political career would be over. Mia confided all this to Ashley, who then told me when she was a little tipsy one night."

"I don't see how this fits into anything," Keri said.

"I don't either. I just thought you should know that Stafford isn't as squeaky clean as he'd like people to think. Personally, I don't like him."

After making sure Britton got safely back to her bedroom, Keri headed back to the station. On the drive she realized something. Mia may have wanted Keri to be heading up the case because they had a bond. But when Stafford backed her up, it wasn't because he thought she was the best person for the job. It was because he thought she was the worst.

If someone was going to end up snooping around in their lives and possibly stumbling on some of their secrets, he wouldn't mind if that someone was a rookie detective, an emotional basket case, someone who'd been reprimanded multiple times in her short career. If things went south, she was the perfect scapegoat. Keri realized she'd walked right into his trap.

And she had a bigger problem. She had no idea what else he was hiding.

CHAPTER FOURTEEN

Monday
Late Night

Pulling back into the parking lot at the station, Keri saw that the media had taken over the place. They swarmed her car until two uniformed officers moved them out of the way enough for her to drive into the lot. Luckily there was a gate separating the employee lot from the general one so they couldn't get too close.

As she walked from her car to the side entrance, blinding flashes of camera lights and shouted questions all merged together. Even if she'd wanted to answer their questions, she couldn't tell them apart from each other. It was all just noise.

Glancing at the digital clock as she entered the bullpen, Keri saw that it was well past eleven. If Ashley really had been abducted in that van right after school, by now she could be as far away as San Francisco, Phoenix, Tijuana, or even Las Vegas.

She walked to her desk, noting that almost no one looked up at her. Some people appeared to be focused intently on their work. But other people seemed to be intentionally avoiding eye contact.

Ray was poring over files at their shared desk. She plopped down in her chair and sighed deeply. Suddenly she felt enormously tired.

"Did that teen Deep Throat have anything earth-shattering to share?" he asked her without looking up.

"She offered some juicy gossip. But nothing that changes things as far as I can tell. What are you up to?"

"Looking at past cases," he said. "Trying to find similar MOs, black vans, whatever."

"Evie's case in there?"

"Yeah, but I skipped it. The pattern didn't seem to match," he said, then finally looked up at her. "Do you disagree?"

"No. This guy was much more careful and deliberate than Evie's abductor. Other than the van, almost nothing else matches up between the cases."

Ray nodded.

"How you doing, Arrietty?" he asked. She could tell he was concerned. She tried to put a brave face on it but she couldn't even think of an insulting nickname comeback.

"I'm okay—just tired and frustrated."

"No missing time lately?"

"Not in the last few hours," she assured him. "I just feel like we keep hitting brick walls. I know that somewhere in all the crap we've been sifting through is an actual clue that will get us to Ashley. But it's hard to see it right now."

"Well, plaster a smile on your face because our fearless leader is headed this way."

Keri looked up to see Lieutenant Hillman walking toward them.

"Anything new, Sands?" he asked brusquely.

"No sir; just looking through old cases for connections."

"Locke, what about you?" he asked, avoiding mentioning the fact that she'd been removed and reinstated on the case within a matter of hours.

"I just met with a friend of Ashley's who said Stafford Penn had an affair with Mia when he was thirty and she was fourteen. She said he's Ashley's father. It might affect his next campaign but I'm not sure how it helps us. Either Artie North or Walker Lee is lying about their interaction but again, I'm not sure that getting the truth on that question gets us any closer to finding Ashley."

"We've got tails on both of them," Hillman told her, "but so far neither one has moved. We're working on getting warrants for the call records of everyone we've interviewed tonight to see if there's anything out of the ordinary but that's still a few hours away. In fact, I'm not sure there's anything either of you can do for now. I recommend you both head home and try to get a few hours of shuteye. I'm going to need you both somewhat fresh to go over those phone LUDs tomorrow morning."

"Maybe I'll just crash in the break room," Keri said.

"That wasn't really a request, Detective Locke. Ashley's former boyfriend, Denton Rivers, is bonding out as we speak and he's been squawking to his lawyer about police brutality. They'll be coming through here in the next five minutes and I don't want a scene where he starts yelling or pointing you out."

"But sir—"

"But nothing. I'm already certain they're going to talk to the press on the way out. I don't need that kid all riled up when he does it. If he sees you, he will be. So go home. I'm leaving in ten minutes myself."

"What's going to happen with that, by the way?" Ray asked.

"My understanding is that his drug dealer, Johnnie Cotton, admitted to assaulting him. Trying to bring a complaint alleging that he was hit in the same spot on his head on the same afternoon by both his dealer and a cop, all while being under suspicion for abducting his girlfriend? Does that sound like a winning case to you?"

"No sir," Ray said, smiling.

"To me either. But the less fuel we add to their fire, the better. That's why I want both of you gone now."

"Yes sir," Ray said, standing up.

"Yes sir," Keri repeated, doing the same. They walked briskly for the exit.

"I'll see you both here at six AM," Hillman shouted after them. "We should have the LUDs by then."

"You want a ride?" Ray asked her. "I know you said you were tired. Just leave your car here. I could even crash at your place...on the couch. We could go in together tomorrow."

"Thanks for the offer but I'm cool. I need to stop at the ladies' room anyway. I'll see you at six."

Ray looked like he wanted to say something else but stopped himself and just nodded.

"See you at six," he agreed and walked out the door to the parking lot.

*

Keri waited in a bathroom stall for fifteen minutes to be sure both Ray and Hillman had left.

When she returned to the bullpen, it was mostly empty. Suarez was still at his desk, typing up reports. Edgerton, the detective who loved all things tech, was doing some kind of cell tower triangulation that Keri didn't completely understand. A detective from Vice was taking a report from a john who said he'd been robbed by the prostitute he'd been with. A homeless guy sat handcuffed to a bench in the corner. He'd defecated on the car hood of a guy he claimed had tossed coffee on him. The car owner, who looked like a real jerk to Keri, seethed as he waited for an officer to take a report. Keri hoped it would be a while.

She made her way back to her desk as unobtrusively as possible and sat down. She wasn't going home. And she knew she wouldn't be able to sleep in the break room, no matter how tired she was. There was a teenage girl in desperate need of her help and she couldn't let her down. Somewhere there was a connection that would solve this case. Keri only hoped she could find it in time.

She grabbed one of the case files on Ray's desk and started rifling through it. There were no obvious similarities. She picked up another one and got more of the same. She slumped back in her chair and closed her eyes for a few seconds. Then she picked up a third file—nothing.

She stood up and headed over to the windows, the same one where she'd watched the mother and daughter pass by earlier in the afternoon. Outside, the night was quiet. It was approaching midnight. All the normal people were home asleep right now. She considered going to the houseboat, even if it was just to zone out to TV for a couple of hours in the hopes of clearing her head.

Just one more file.

She headed back to the desk and picked one up at random. A ten-year-old black girl named London Jaquet disappeared walking home from school and was never heard from again. That was six years ago. Technically the case was "open" but some pages were stuck together because they hadn't been touched in so long.

Similarities to Ashley: female, after school, young.

Similarities to Evie: female, never heard from again, elementary school age.

Keri set the file to the side and picked up another one. It was for a forty-four-year-old Hispanic man who went missing two years ago. His tattoos indicated gang affiliations. The file was thin. No one had worked it all that hard. Keri set it to the side and picked up another one.

A six-year-old Korean girl named Vanda Kang disappeared from the back seat of a car when her mother stepped into a mom-and-pop liquor store on Centinela Avenue to buy a pack of cigarettes. Seven years later, at age thirteen, the girl was found alive and healthy, living with a wealthy white couple in Seattle who claimed they'd adopted her.

A man named Thomas Anderson, aka The Ghost, had only recently been identified as the abductor, eighteen months ago, in fact. He actually went to trial, defended himself even. The file said that if the evidence hadn't been so overwhelming he might have gotten off. He was very convincing in the courtroom. He was currently finishing up the first year of a ten-year sentence. He was supposed to be doing his time at Folsom State Prison, but because of overcrowding he was still being held in county lockup at the Twin Towers Correctional Facility in downtown LA. Keri had been there on a few occasions. She didn't love it.

She sat in her chair, swiveling back and forth, turning an idea over and over in her mind.

The Ghost is a professional kidnapper. It's a business. And a business like this requires clients, and co-workers, and middlemen. It required an entire network of connections.

Maybe she'd been going at this all wrong. If this was a professional job, and the video from that bail bonds camera sure made it look like one, why was she talking to boyfriends and drug dealers?

If I'm going to catch a pro, I need to talk to a pro.

Keri stood up, grabbed her bag, and headed for the door. Suarez glanced up, zombie-eyed, and nodded. The homeless guy blew her a kiss. She winked at him and walked out the door. It was after midnight now. That meant it was a new day. And a new day meant a fresh start. And what better way to start than with a ghost.

CHAPTER FIFTEEN

Tuesday
Wee Hours

When Keri entered the windowless concrete room at the Twin Towers, she looked at the man who had been pulled out of his cell and dragged there in the middle of the night. He was sitting down so she couldn't gauge his height, but he appeared to be in his early fifties. Still, she was more than glad that his wrists were chained to the steel table. Even wearing loose prison clothes, the Ghost projected a still, coiled strength.

Every visible part of his right side was covered in tattoos, from fingertips up his neck to his earlobe. The left side didn't have a single one. His thick black hair was parted neatly. His dark eyes gleamed with curiosity. He waited patiently for her, not saying a word.

Keri slid into the fixed bench seat on the other side of the table and did her best to hide her uneasiness. She considered how to proceed before deciding to start with more honey than vinegar.

"Good morning," she said. "I'm sorry to get you out of bed at such a late hour, but I was hoping you could help me. I'm Detective Keri Locke with LAPD Missing Persons."

"What can I do for you, Detective?" he purred, as if he'd been awake and expecting her this whole time."

"You snatched that little Korean girl on behalf of a Seattle couple," she said. "It was a job for hire."

"That's what I was convicted of," he said coolly.

Keri leaned forward.

"What I want to know is, how did those people find you?"

"Ask them."

Keri pressed, saying, "I mean, here they were, seemingly upstanding people, but they were somehow able to find you. How does that connection get made?"

"Why do you ask?"

Keri debated how forthright to be with this guy. She got the sense that if she played the usual cat and mouse games, he'd just shut down. And she didn't have time for that.

"I'm working on a case. A fifteen-year-old girl was abducted yesterday after school. Every second counts. There's a chance that the man who did it was hired, just like you were. How would he have been contacted? How did they find him?"

The Ghost thought for a moment.

"Do you think I could get a cup of green tea? I find it very soothing."

"Milk or sugar?" Keri asked.

"Neither," he answered, leaning back as much as his cuffs would allow.

Keri nodded to the guard, who muttered something unintelligible into his walkie-talkie.

"You're asking me to betray a confidence, Detective Locke. That's a big deal in a place like this. If it got out, I could be at risk."

"Somehow I think you know how to handle yourself."

"Be that as it may, I need some assurances from you that my assistance will be reciprocated."

"Mr. Anderson, if your information is useful in the case, I'm going to write a nice, long letter to the parole board on your behalf, explaining how cooperative you were with me tonight. My understanding is that right now, you're not even up for a hearing for four more years. Is that right?"

"You've been doing your research," he noted, his eyes twinkling with delight.

"Why do I think I'm not the only one?" she said. The tea arrived in a sad little white Styrofoam cup. As he sipped, Keri couldn't help but ask the question that had been eating at her.

"You seem like a smart man, Mr. Anderson. How is it that you were caught along with so much evidence that, even with your powers of persuasion, you were still convicted?"

The Ghost swallowed luxuriously before responding. Something about the way he carried himself made Keri wonder what this guy's background was. She was so focused on the task at hand, it hadn't occurred to her to look much beyond his rap sheet. But he didn't have the bearing of any criminal she'd met before. She made a mental note to look into it when time allowed.

"That is suspicious, isn't it? How can you be certain, Detective, that things didn't play out exactly as I anticipated? That I'm not exactly where I want to be right now?"

"That sounds like a guy trying to cover for a plan that went south."

"It does, doesn't it?" he said, smiling, exposing a mouth of perfectly white teeth.

"So, to business then?" Keri prompted.

"One last thing before we begin. If I assist you and you don't live up to your end of the bargain, that's the kind of thing a man like me might remember for a long time. It's the kind of thing that might keep me up at night."

"I hope you're not threatening me, Mr. Anderson," she said with more confidence than she felt.

"Of course not. I'm just saying it would make me sad."

"Noted. You have my word," Keri said, and meant it. "But I'm working off a ticking clock here so it's time for you to be helpful now."

"Very well. How do the connections get made? Sometimes it's as simple as Craigslist or the online editions of local weeklies. But mostly it's through the dark web. You're familiar, I gather?"

Keri nodded. The dark web was an online underground marketplace where buyers and sellers of various criminal endeavors could find each other. Anderson continued.

"If people know what they're doing, these transactions are almost impossible to trace. Every keystroke is encrypted with state of the art technology. Once you're in the community, you can communicate freely. One could be as direct as saying, "Looking to have my uncle disappear, Glendale, within two weeks." Without an encryption key, nobody can ever identify you, including the people who reply to your post. That anonymity works both ways. Once interest has been established, additional communication usually occurs in the real world through anonymous e-mail or burner cell phones via a pre-established code."

Keri wasn't impressed.

"I already know most of this." she said. "What I need from you are specifics—the names of colleagues who might do a job like the one I'm investigating. I need a lead."

"I can't offer you Christian names, Detective Locke. It doesn't work like that. Everybody has a nickname like mine."

"The Ghost?"

"Yes. It may seem silly but we refer to each other by them as well. Our proper names only get used if we're caught."

"So how does a potential client connect with one of you?"

"A lot of it is run through defense lawyers," he said. "They end up defending people who get caught. Their clients tell them who's in the game; those communications are protected under the attorney-client privilege. Lawyers talk to other lawyers, ostensibly for help on their cases, so the privilege stays attached, and the names spread. As we speak, there are lawyers throughout California who could tell you the names of a dozen people who would take an abduction-for-hire assignment, or even a murder for hire. And of course, it's all privileged."

It made sense from a logistics point of view but it seemed too bizarre to actually be true.

"Not if they're setting up connections," Keri said. "Then they're criminals themselves and the privilege goes away."

The man shrugged.

"How would you ever know about it?"

"Does your lawyer set up deals?"

The man smiled.

"Answering that question would not be in my self-interest. All I can say is that my attorney is well connected, as any self-respecting barrister should be."

This guy is a piece of work.

"Give me some nicknames, Mr. Anderson."

"No can do."

The words were clear but there was a hesitation in them. He was clearly thinking about that parole letter.

"Okay, forget names. Are you familiar with a guy who worked this area about five years ago? Drove a black van, blond with a tattoo on the right side of his neck?"

"That physical description matches half the guys in this place. I myself have an affinity for skin art," he said, leaning in so she could get a better look at the tattoo on his own neck.

"What about the van?"

"That narrows things down quite a bit. There's no way to be sure but the man you described might be someone they call the Collector. I don't know his real name and quite frankly I don't want to. I've never personally met him or even seen him for that matter."

"What *do* you know about him?"

"Word is, he can be commissioned for murders for hire. That's not his main business though. His primary work is the abduction and sale of people, usually children."

For sale.

The words sent a chill down Keri's spine. Was Evie stolen only to be sold to the highest bidder? In some weird way, it was almost comforting. At least then there was the chance that someone actually wanted her to be part of their family, just like with that Korean girl in Seattle. But if she was just randomly taken and put up for sale, there was no telling who would buy her, or for what reason.

Keri forced herself to focus, shaking herself out of the trance. How long had she been out of it? Two seconds? Twenty? She glanced at Anderson, who was smiling patiently. Had he noticed anything? The guard was oblivious, reading a text on his phone.

She tried to regain her focus.

"How do I get in touch with him, this Collector?"

"You don't."

"How do I find out about his upcoming sales?"

"Someone like you, you don't."

"Where does he operate out of? What city?"

"I couldn't say. I know he's been credited with jobs throughout California, Arizona, and Nevada. I'm sure that's not all."

"What's your lawyer's name—the one who defended you at trial?"

"It's in the court file."

"I know it's in the court file. Save me some time. It'll help with your parole letter."

Anderson hesitated a moment. He reminded her of a chess player thinking ten moves ahead.

"Jackson Cave," he finally said.

Keri knew the name.

Jackson Cave was one of the city's most prominent defense lawyers. His boutique downtown firm was located near the top of the US Bank Tower near the convention center. It was in a nice location but was also conveniently located within a ten-minute drive of this very facility.

Keri stood up.

"Thanks for your time, Mr. Anderson. I'll get to that letter when I get some downtime."

"I appreciate that, Detective."

"Enjoy the rest of your evening," she said as she headed for the door.

"I'll do my best," he replied, then added just before she left, "One more thing."

"Yes?"

"I would tell you not to contact Mr. Cave but I know that would be useless. I'm sure you will. However, I would ask that you leave my name out of it. I have a long memory for slights. But his is even longer."

"Good night," she said, without agreeing to anything. As she walked down the hall, even though they were separated by a wall, Keri could swear she felt the Ghost's eyes on her.

*

Back in the car, as she headed toward the station, Keri tried to force the image of Thomas Anderson from her mind and fixate on what he'd said.

The Collector. Was that the man who'd taken Evie? Had he taken Ashley as well?

She plugged the nickname into her vehicle computer while idling at a light. Over thirty cases came up, just in California. Was he really responsible for that many abductions or did lazy detectives just decide to use him as a boogeyman if they couldn't make any headway on their cases? She noticed that nowhere in the system did it list a proper name, a photograph, or an arrest.

She was pretty sure there was someone who could identify him but she doubted he'd be very forthcoming. His name was Jackson Cave. Keri wanted desperately to drive to his home, pound on his door, and begin interrogating him. But she knew she couldn't and that it wouldn't do any good.

When she came at Jackson Cave, keeper of secrets for child abductors, she wanted to be on top of her game. But right now she was exhausted and disoriented. Not only was that not good for a confrontation with Cave, it wasn't helping Ashley Penn either.

Keri jacked up the air conditioning all the way in the hopes that it would clear her head. Even approaching one in the morning, the temperature gauge said it was eighty-eight degrees outside. When would this heat ever break?

And if she was sweating through her shirt, Keri could only imagine what Ashley was going through. Was she still in the back of some stifling van? Bound up somewhere in a closet? Being abused in some sweaty back room?

Wherever she was, it was Keri's responsibility to find her. It had been almost ten hours since she'd disappeared. Experience had taught her that every second missing was a second closer to death. She had to find a new lead—or maybe an old one. Who had lied to her since this case began? Who had been hiding the most?

And then it came to her. There was someone. She wouldn't be going straight back to the station. Keri would be making a pit stop first.

CHAPTER SIXTEEN

Tuesday
Wee Hours

Sweat poured down Ashley's face as she scanned the walls in a controlled panic. It had to be twenty-five degrees hotter in this metal tube than outside.

She looked up. Four or five feet above her head, at the top of the silo, was a large metal hatch, three feet by five feet, closed shut. The hinges were on the outside. She must have, she realized, been brought in here through that hatch. That meant there must be some type of fixed ladder going up the side of the silo to get to that door. If she could get through it, then there might be a way down to the ground.

She jumped and grazed it with her fingertips—barely.

She climbed the plastic bin, reaching—but it suddenly collapsed under her weight.

She stood again, frustrated. What she needed was a long stick. Maybe it would flip open if she could get some pressure on it.

Then again, maybe it was padlocked on the outside.

A long stick...

She looked around. The wooden boards of the flooring might actually be long enough if she could get one loose.

How?

They were screwed down.

Nothing in her tub of goodies could be used as a screwdriver.

Then she saw it: the cans of soup had pull-tabs. She pulled a top off, set the soup to the side, and wiggled the pull-tab back and forth until it broke off from the lid.

She found that all the screws were sunken into the wood a quarter inch or so, not far in but far enough that the pull-tab couldn't grab the screws' surface.

She had an idea. After eating the soup (why let it go to waste?) she scraped away at the wood around a screw with the edge of the can. It was hard going but she eventually got the head of the screw exposed enough that she could get the pull-tab into the thread. Holding the pull-tab as tight as she could and pressing down with force, she was actually able to get the screw moving.

It took a long time, fifteen minutes at least, to get it all the way out. There were ten screws in that board.

The project would take two and a half hours if the muscles in her hand held out, longer if she took breaks. Actually, if she left the last two screws at the end of the board, she might be able to lift it from the opposite side and force them out. That would bring it down to two hours. The flashlight should hold out that long.

There'd be no magic marker on the walls from her.

I'm getting the hell out of here!

*

Ignoring the silent suffocating air of the silo for what seemed like an eternity, Ashley slowly removed one screw after another. She could picture herself prying open the ceiling door, then jumping up and grabbing the lip, muscling herself up and through, then going down the ladder and running away into the night where she couldn't be found.

The moment of truth was finally here.

She got the board vertical, yanked it loose from the last remaining screws, raised it until it rested against the edge of the hatch, and pushed.

Nothing happened.

She pushed up with all her might; nothing. She pounded the plank against the hatch with all the power she could summon. It didn't budge an inch. It was solidly latched shut from the outside.

Ashley slumped to the ground, worn out and beaten. She curled up in a ball and closed her eyes, ready to meet whatever fate was in store for her. But then a memory snuck into her mind, of another time she had felt defeated.

While surfing in Hawaii two years ago, a wave far bigger than any she'd encountered in Southern California had overwhelmed her. At least twenty feet high, it had slammed her into a coral bed fifteen feet down on the ocean floor. Her bodysuit had snagged on a sharp piece of coral. She couldn't escape.

She struggled but knew she was running out of breath. Then a second wave came, smashing her even deeper into the coral. She felt it cutting into her flesh. But this time, when the wave passed, she found that it had somehow freed her from the coral she'd been stuck on.

With her last ounce of strength she'd pushed herself to the surface, her eyes aimed squarely on the dot of sunlight growing ever closer. Her first breath of air upon breaking the surface remained the most powerful moment of her life. It was better than any drug she'd taken, any guy she'd slept with. It was her true north.

And if she'd found it once, Ashley knew she could find it again.

She sat up.

She fished around and found the flashlight, shining it down into the opening where the board had been. Below the wooden platform she was on, there was some kind of giant rusty funnel. The walls sloped down into a spout that was about two feet in diameter.

Could her body fit through it? It would be close. She might slide through. She might get wedged in and get stuck. It was hard to tell.

It looked like something might be jammed in part of the spout, four or five feet into it. What was it? Spider webs? Old rotted clumps of grain? It wasn't a solid blockage and certainly wasn't part of the structure itself. It looked fragile, as if the weight of her body could crush it. Still, she couldn't be sure and she couldn't see past it.

She dropped the empty soup can down.

It rattled against the spout as it bumped up against the blockage, then passed through and fell to the ground. It took a while to hit the bottom. The drop was a long one.

Sweat ran down Ashley's face.

If she pulled another board out, there would be enough room for her to drop down into the funnel. It was possible—maybe—that she'd fit through the spout without getting wedged in, then fall to the ground below without breaking her back and killing herself, and then find that there was a door or opening of some sort that she could escape through.

It was equally possible that she'd get wedged into the spout, inextricably stuck and unable to move. Her own weight might squeeze her in tight and constrict her chest. She might suffocate or worse, forever be on the verge of suffocating while never actually getting there.

She wouldn't be able to kill herself. She'd die a horrible, immobile death.

She screamed at the top of her lungs and beat the side of the silo with the board. The frustration was too much.

"Help me! Somebody help me! I didn't do anything!"

She stuck the board down into the spout and was just able to reach the blockage. As she moved it around and poked at it, she realized, with horror, what it was.

Bones.

Bones covered with years of dust and cobwebs and stale air. Someone had already tried her idea of dropping down and had gotten wedged in.

Ashley scurried away from the sight until the wall stopped her. She didn't want to die like that. It was too horrible.

Tears came to her eyes. There was no way out—not up, not down. She was stuck. The fear took over again.

"Mommy!" she screamed. "Help me!"

CHAPTER SEVENTEEN

Tuesday
1 AM

Keri's eyes were heavy as she drove from downtown back to Venice. At 1 AM on a Tuesday morning, the typically brutal Los Angeles traffic was a breeze, but she was in no mood to appreciate it. She realized she was drifting across the lane on Lincoln Boulevard and yanked herself back. She jacked up the radio on some awful-sounding EDM song and lowered all her windows, letting the hot nighttime air whip at her face and hair.

Someone was lying to her. The stories of boy toy rocker Walker Lee and security guard Artie North were completely at odds. But without evidence to go on, she had to depend on her instincts.

That's why she was pulling up next to Lee's apartment. She considered calling Ray but decided he could use the sleep. Besides, if things went south, this would be better as a solo project.

She banged on his door and he answered within seconds. Clearly he hadn't been sleeping. A suitcase sat open on the couch behind him. It was stuffed to the brim.

Keri looked at it, then at him, and said, "I talked to the security guard, Artie North. He denied having any footage of Ashley or using anything like that to try to extort her into sex."

Walker rolled his eyes.

"The little shit's lying."

"Even if that's true, the more I mull it over, the more I think you pointed me to him as a decoy. There's something going on you haven't told me about. I told you before, be straight with me and you won't have anything to worry about. But lie to me..." She let the sentence trail off.

Walker Lee stood in the doorway, clearly unsure how to proceed. Keri tried to help him out. She nodded at the suitcase.

"Are you leaving town?"

"Yes."

"When?"

"Any minute, actually."

She tried to bite her tongue but couldn't. "That's a pretty pathetic thing to do, don't you think? With Ashley needing everyone in her corner right now?"

His eyes got stony.

"You know what? Enough's enough. I'm sorry if something's happened to Ashley but I'm sick of you being here."

Keri was surprised by the defiance in his tone. He'd played it so cool up to now that she'd been taken in. But he was definitely hiding something. She just wasn't sure if it had something to do with Ashley's disappearance.

"Mind if I come in?" she asked after she brushed past him and was already well into the apartment.

Despite her rising blood pressure, she walked quickly but calmly back to his studio. He tried to keep up, futilely saying, "I do mind."

Ashley moved to the microphone stand in the middle of the room, slowly removed the mic, and stared at it introspectively, as if she'd never seen one before. Then she suddenly swung it by the cord, in a circle high above her head, allowing the frustration of the day to fuel her. Walker Lee stared for a moment, dumbfounded. Then he found his wits again and opened his mouth.

Hey, don't—" he started. But before he could finish the sentence, Keri changed the trajectory of the microphone and swung it at him. It struck him flush on the forehead above the left eye.

He slumped to the floor, dazed. After a moment, he reached up to the spot and then looked at his hand. It was covered in blood, which was flowing profusely down his cheek onto his bare chest.

It took a second for what had happened to register. While Keri waited for him to process it, she walked over to the counter and grabbed a rag she found lying there. She tossed it in his general direction.

"What did you do to my face?" he whined pathetically.

Keri knew she'd probably gone too far but she was committed at this point. She felt wide awake now.

"I'm sick of you screwing around with me. We're done with that. Get it?"

The man put the rag to the wound to stanch the bleeding and said, "I'm going to sue you."

"The only thing you're going to do is tell me what I need to know, Walker. Otherwise, the other side of your head's going to get a matching welt. Or maybe I'll go for your guitar-playing hand next. You lured me into this soundproof studio and came at me. I defended myself forcefully. That's the story everyone will believe unless you start talking *right now*."

Whatever he'd been hiding this whole time, Keri could tell he was about to finally give it up.

"Look, the only other thing I can think of is, there's this guy who hangs out near the Boardwalk that me and Ashley buy drugs from now and then; nothing serious, just pot and ecstasy. He goes by the name Auggie."

Keri had never heard of him before. Either he was small-time or it was an alias.

"Okay, go on."

"Well, the last time we did business with him—when was it? Wednesday night, yeah, that's it—he was looking at Ashley really weird the whole time, like a wolf looking at a bunny or something. I didn't say anything but I can tell you I didn't like it. He gave us the stuff, I gave him the money, but then he wanted more. He said the price had gone up. He told me to come back with the rest of the money within the next few days. Then he made a cryptic remark, which I took to be a vague threat against Ashley if I didn't return to pay him more. I never went back. Screw him, it wasn't fair. He jacked up the price without telling me. I don't play those kinds of games. Also, I heard his guys use a van for smashing and grabbing TVs and computers and stuff. Don't know the color though."

Keri tried to imagine it. If Walker was telling the truth, then Ashley knew Auggie and wouldn't hesitate to move closer to a van he was in.

"You should have told me this before."

"What I should have done before was never get Ashley involved in all this stupid stuff to begin with," he admitted. "I should have kept her safe. I don't know how all this got so screwed up."

Keri looked at him closely. The left side of his face was covered in blood-matted blond hair. But she sensed something approaching sincerity. Maybe there was hope for him yet. But that wasn't her concern.

"Do you know where Auggie lives?"

"No. But he hangs out in a dive club called the Blue Mist Lounge, at Windward and Pacific, right next to Townhouse. That's where everybody meets up with him."

That was only half a mile from Ashley's house. Keri pulled five twenties from her purse, tossed them on the floor, and said, "Go get that head stitched up. There's an urgent care clinic ten blocks east of here." She paused and added, "And don't trip into any more counters."

He nodded, understanding. And then he surprised her.

"Be careful with Auggie, Detective. He's a seriously bad guy."

"Thanks," she said as she walked out, not saying out loud what was going through her mind.

I'm feeling seriously bad myself right about now.

CHAPTER EIGHTEEN

Tuesday
Wee Hours

Keri called Ray on her way over. She didn't want to but the Blue Mist Lounge was the kind of place that required backup.

"Sleeping?" she asked.

"I was," he snapped, sounding not too happy.

A pause.

"You're not," he realized. "And you need me."

"Bingo," she said.

He sighed audibly.

"And if you need me, it must be bad."

"Right again," she said.

"I hate you, Locke."

"I love you, Big."

He sighed audibly. There came a creaking noise, and she knew he was sitting up in bed.

"You're lucky I'm alone this time," he said. "What's the address?"

Fifteen minutes later, Keri pulled up in front of the Blue Mist and waited, knowing Ray would be there any minute. While she waited, she glanced over Auggie's rap sheet. He was a small-time crook and dealer but had a big-time temper. He'd spent sixteen of his thirty-four years incarcerated, mostly for assaults. There was no record of abductions but he had once kept a girlfriend locked in a bedroom closet for twelve hours because he thought she'd stolen some meth from him.

Ray showed up and she got out of the car and stood beside him.

He looked at the club.

"The Blue Mist, huh?" he asked. "Knew I could count on you to invite me to a classy date."

They approached the door silently, Ray stiffening, clearly, she knew, preparing for trouble.

Waiting for them at the front door of the club was a pit bull of a guard. But they flashed their badges and after he took one look at Ray, he stepped aside.

They pushed their way past him and up the stairs to the entrance. Loud hip-hop music blasted from the speakers. Keri noted that she was the only white person in the place and felt a little guilty at being relieved that Ray was by her side.

They moved quickly to the back VIP room, which had its own security guard. Ray nodded at him and showed his badge and he stepped aside as they entered.

The door closed behind them, blocking out the music from the main room. In here, a woman on a small stage in the corner was singing Billie Holiday. It was much busier than Keri expected at this hour early in the week.

They looked around. Ray nodded to a darkened corner of the room and muttered, "Mr. Dreadlocks."

Auggie sat in a large booth away from the crowd. Two women sat on either side of him. Keri recognized them both as working girls. They were snuggled in close, competing for his attention. A bottle of whiskey sat in the middle of the table, half empty, with glasses all around. The women laughed loudly at everything Auggie said and none of them noticed Ray and Keri walking over until they were at the table.

Ray slid in next to one of the women, who was wearing a low-cut red top. Keri remained standing.

"Hey, folks," he said pleasantly.

At first the woman looked taken aback, but once she got a good look at him, she smiled. Keri ignored the uncomfortable feeling of being slightly jealous of a prostitute.

Auggie didn't speak but his whole body had tensed up, reminding Keri of a coiled rattlesnake.

Suddenly the woman on the other side of him, who wore a too-tight tube top, slammed her hand on the table and said, "You're the Sandman!"

The woman next to Ray didn't understand.

"The Sandman! The boxer!"

Tube Top swung around to Ray's side and slid in until her thigh was fully pressed against his, putting him in a hooker sandwich.

"I can't believe the Sandman's in here!" she nearly shouted with joy.

Keri had been watching Auggie closely. In the space of about ten seconds, his expression had silently gone from suspicious to envious to fearful. And then she saw something flash across his face that she couldn't quite identify. It wasn't until he had jumped up onto the table and leapt down in the direction of the exit that she realized what it was: desperation.

Auggie was quick but Keri had been anticipating something from him and moved over to shoulder check him when his feet landed on the ground. He saw what she was doing and adjusted in mid-air so that they would collide directly, his nearly two hundred pound frame slamming into her. She was giving up nearly seventy pounds to him and knew that even though she was well positioned, she was going to take the brunt of the impact.

She was right.

His body pounded into hers with a force that knocked her off her feet and sent her rolling back across the floor. The back of her head slammed hard on the wooden floor but she used the backward momentum to roll in a backward somersault and pop right back up. She was upright but colors exploded behind her eyes as her skull screamed.

She realized half a second too late that she was directly in Auggie's exit path and that he planned to go through instead of around her. She bent at the knees to avoid becoming a tackling dummy but it didn't help much. He smashed into her and as they both fell, his knee landed in her gut, knocking the wind out of her. She felt the bile rise in her throat as she gasped for breath. Auggie scrambled to his feet and darted out the door.

From her prone position on the floor, Keri saw Ray desperately disentangling himself from the hookers and the booth. He ran to her but she used what little strength she had to wave for him to go after Auggie. He nodded and barreled through the door after his prey.

Keri lay there for a few seconds, gulping down air. As she rolled over and started to get up, she felt arms on her shoulder, helping pull her to her feet. It was Red Top and Tube Top. She nodded her thanks, still unable to speak, and stumbled out the door after Ray and Auggie.

"Which way?" she mumbled to the security guard. He pointed at the back entrance. She ran over to it and shoved open the door, which led to a rickety metal stairway in the club's back alley. She heard voices.

In the distance, she saw that Ray had Auggie trapped against a fence. The suspect tried to climb it but lost his grip and slipped down to the ground. Ray had been chasing him and was only ten feet away when Auggie whirled around with a gun in his hand. He fired.

Ray kept coming.

Auggie fired again right as Ray leapt onto him. They collapsed in a heap and Keri could no longer tell what was going on. She scurried down the steps, made the six-foot leap from the last step to the street below, and ran in the direction of the men. She was halfway there when she realized what was happening.

Both of Auggie's shots had missed. Ray had landed on top of him, pinned him down, and was proceeding to pummel the shit out of him. Auggie's face was a pulpy mess. He wasn't moving.

"Ray, stop!" she shouted. "We need him alive!"

Her words seemed to shake him out of his trance and he stopped punching. He rolled off Auggie onto his back and lay there on the asphalt, sucking in huge breaths.

Keri ran over and looked into Auggie's bloody swollen eyes. He was conscious. His breath was shallow but he was breathing.

"Hi, Auggie." she said. "We just stopped by to talk to you about one of your clients, a girl named Ashley Penn."

The man said nothing.

"But now you're under arrest for the attempted murder of a police officer. This could have gone so differently."

The man winced in pain and wheezed one word: "Cooperate."

Keri rolled him roughly over onto his stomach and yanked his arms behind his back to cuff him.

"Oh, you better believe you're going to cooperate, Auggie. Otherwise, this was just round one with the Sandman."

CHAPTER NINETEEN

From behind the glass of the observation room, Keri, Ray, and Hillman watched as Auggie paced back and forth in Interrogation Room 1. Nobody had said a word to him in the forty-five minutes since Keri had promised him that his health depended on his cooperation. Multiple detectives, black-and-whites, and CSIs were down at the Blue Mist Lounge, processing the alley where a suspect had shot at an officer. Auggie was screwed. He was facing about a dozen charges, not the least of which was attempted murder. Everyone wanted to make it stick.

Hillman looked at Keri. She knew he was pissed about having to come back to the station in the middle of the night.

"You got five minutes, max. If the guy even says the word "lawyer," I want you to immediately stop talking and leave the room. I want this guy off the streets and that means we're going to play it strictly by the book. Just having him here right now instead of at the ER is a risk. I don't want some sleazy defense lawyer wiggling him free. Do we understand each other?"

"Yes, sir."

Keri took a second to tuck in her shirt and make sure the hair was out of her face. She had a massive headache and possibly a cracked rib. But she didn't want Auggie to think he'd made even a dent.

She walked into the interrogation room and said, "Remember me?"

Auggie started to say something but Keri waved him to a halt. "Don't say the word lawyer. If you do I have to stop talking and then I can't help you."

Auggie scoffed at her.

"You two never identified yourselves," he said. "I thought you were there to rob me or something. That's why I ran. Out in the alley, when I shot, that was total self-defense. I have a license for the gun. You can check it out. I didn't do nothing wrong."

Keri rolled her eyes.

"Look, you're going to spend some time in jail, that's just the way things are. But whether that time turns out to be five or fifty years may very well depend on how many friends you make around here in the next five minutes. So here's your one and only chance. Tell me about Ashley Penn."

Auggie didn't need to be told twice.

"I never personally sold anything to her, or to anyone, for that matter."

It was a lie but Keri let it slide. She sensed there was more coming.

"But...?"

"But I heard a rumor that she did frequent the neighborhood now and then, if you know what I mean. I also heard a rumor that she recently made a very large purchase because she was going to head to a different state. She wanted a reserve until she could find a hook-up there."

"Which state?"

"I don't know."

"Who was she going with?"

"I don't know."

"Was it a long-haired guy?"

"I know who you mean. That rock star guy," Auggie said. "No, it wasn't him. Rumor was that it was with one of her girlfriends."

This is new. Did Ashley have a side piece and Walker found out? He wouldn't like that.

"Can you describe this girl?" she asked.

"Nah, man, all I know is rumors. That girl had a lot of rumors about her."

Keri left the room. Hillman had given her five minutes and she'd used less than two.

Her mind raced.

Could Walker have learned about the plan and tried to put a stop to it? Could he have pulled Ashley into the van, initially just to talk her out of leaving, but then, maybe things escalated afterward? Maybe things got violent? Walker didn't have an alibi. But he didn't have a van either.

She stood outside the interrogation room, turning the options over in her head until Hillman and Ray came out of the observation room to join her.

"There you go. She ran away," Hillman said.

Keri doubted it.

"Maybe she was planning to but I don't think that's what happened."

"Why not?"

"The girl who got in that van didn't look like she was going on some big trip," she said.

Hillman shook his head.

"Maybe she and this mystery girl were headed to the place where they loaded up for the trip. Didn't Walker Lee say she was considering faking her own abduction?"

"He did. But he said she wasn't serious. It's not impossible but it just doesn't feel right. Everything about this case feels like an abduction."

Hillman sighed deeply. She could tell he was trying not to lose his cool.

"It's almost three in the morning. We've been going at this thing nonstop for over ten hours and we don't have anything firm to indicate that she was taken as opposed to leaving on her own. Unfortunately for you, Detective Locke, we don't pursue cases based on how they feel. So this gut feeling you have isn't enough to go on."

She needed him on her side so Keri fought the urge to come back at him too hard.

"It's more than just my gut, sir."

"Then what?"

"I don't know," Keri said. "I can't think right now."

"Exactly," Hillman said. "We're all zombies. What that means is that we're all going home now to get some rest, which is what you should have done in the first place. That's an order." He focused on Keri and repeated the words. "That's an order."

"Okay," she said.

"Sleep," he repeated, before adding, "but I want everyone back here at seven in the morning."

*

Before heading home, Keri made a quick stop at her desk. She wanted to run both Thomas "The Ghost" Anderson and the defense lawyer, Jackson Cave, through the databases to see if anything magically popped up. She was curious about Anderson but time was short so she decided to focus on Cave, who was more immediately relevant right now. There was lots of info but nothing immediately incriminating.

Still, she couldn't help but suspect that Cave might have information on the Collector. He might even have a real name. Keri had to find out. But how?

Even if she broke into his office it wasn't like he'd have a file in a cabinet labeled "abductors for hire." This was the kind of information that he kept safely tucked away in his head. And she needed to find a way to access it. Maybe she could find some dirt on him, something that would get him disbarred if he didn't cooperate with her. Blackmail was a useful tool.

She sighed heavily and lost her focus briefly. Almost instantly, thoughts of Evie flooded her head. She saw the expression of terror on her daughter's face as she looked back at her mother that day in the park, her little body clutched in a stranger's arms. She heard the cries in her head.

"Mommy! Mommy!"

She felt tears coming to her eyes and rushed to the restroom before anyone could notice. Once in a stall, she let go, allowing the silent sobs to wrack her body. She sat on the bathroom floor for five minutes before she trusted herself to get up.

When she stepped out of the restroom, Ray was waiting for her. He put his arms around her.

"I thought you went home," she said.

"Well, it looks like I didn't. You want me to stay with you?"

She considered it for half a second.

"No, I'm okay."

"You sure?"

"No." She smiled and said, "Ray, am I ever going to be okay?"

"You're already okay," he said. "It's just going to take some more time to work all the way through it."

"I don't want to work through it. I want to find Evie."

"You will," he said. "*We* will. What you need to do is stay strong until then. Okay?"

She leaned into his hug.

"You're good people, Jolly Green Giant."

"You too, Thumbelina," he said. "Did I say thanks for stopping me before I killed Auggie?"

"No."

"Thank you," he said.

Five minutes later Keri was in the Prius. She was both exhausted and tingling with raw energy. She knew she had to go home to crash for a couple of hours if she was going to make any sense of this case. But before she did, there was one small thing she needed to do first.

CHAPTER TWENTY

Tuesday
Wee Hours

Fighting the urge to sleep, Keri drove by West Venice High. She'd heard rumors that there was a vigil going on. She parked near the front entrance and walked over. It was hard to miss. About forty students and teachers stood on the grassy clearing below the main steps, lighting candles, holding hands, and talking about Ashley. Some chatted quietly among themselves. Others spoke dramatically for the cameras from local stations that had set up shop onsite. A few uniformed officers stood off to the side, leaning against the hood of their black-and-white, taking it all in.

Keri moved among them as unobtrusively as possible. These people might be willing to talk, especially outside the intimidating confines of a police station. Maybe she could learn something of value from casual conversations that formal interviews might miss.

Ashley's third-period geometry teacher, Lex Hartley, a balding fifty-something potato of a man, said Ashley was a good kid, a normal kid, although he had to admit her grades had dropped lately.

"Tell me about Artie North."

Hartley looked surprised.

"Why? Is he involved?"

"I'm just following up on some rumors. Did you ever hear any rumors that he was extorting Ashley for sex?"

"Absolutely not. I've known Artie for five years. He's a good guy, a little lonely maybe. But he takes protecting these kids seriously."

"A month or so ago, did he get beat up?"

"Yeah. He has a second job doing security work down at a Metrolink maintenance yard. A couple of homeless guys attacked him when he was trying to get them off the grounds."

"That's what he told you?"

"Yes."

"How banged up was he?"

"I don't know...a purple eye, a busted lip."

In the ongoing war of conflicting stories between Artie North and Walker Lee, Keri wondered if she'd ever learn the truth.

She pressed on through the crowd, gathering snippets of information from forthcoming students.

A girl named Clarice Brown said that Ashley had been learning how to shoot a gun. She said it was for protection but wasn't clear on whether she was protecting herself or someone else. She quietly whispered that Ashley had been doing a lot of drugs lately. To get the money, she'd been taking her mother's jewelry out of the vault and pawning it.

Miranda Sanchez, the girl who originally saw Ashley enter the van, was there too. She said that a lot of the girls at school were jealous bitches who hated Ashley. They started all kinds of rumors. You never knew what was true about Ashley or what was totally bogus made-up crap spawned by haters. Personally, she liked Ashley.

A junior named Sean Ringer said that Ashley told him a couple of weeks ago that her dad, the senator, was in some kind of trouble. Ashley hadn't elaborated but seemed sincere when she said it, maybe even a little scared.

Out of the corner of her eye, Keri saw sudden movement in her direction. A reporter from KTLA had spotted her and was rushing over with a camera crew in tow. She turned her back, put on the baseball cap she'd kept in her back pocket for just this circumstance, and quickly weaved her way through the crowd, back toward the car. She heard a shouted question about thirty feet behind her.

"Detective Locke, is it true that the FBI has taken over the Ashley Penn investigation?"

She kept moving, saying nothing, walking as fast as she could without breaking into a run.

*

Back in the car on the way to the houseboat, Keri tried to process everything that had been thrown at her in the last few minutes.

Had the FBI taken over the investigation? She wanted to call Hillman but thought better of it at 3:30 in the morning.

She tried to sift rumor from fact. Ashley had bought a gun? Artie North *had* been beaten up by someone? Ashley was pawning jewelry? Senator Penn was in some kind of trouble?

Instead of getting solid leads, all she had now were more questions, almost none of which had easy answers. She realized too late that she'd only made things worse by going to the school. If she'd just gone straight home, she'd be asleep by now. Instead, she was driving through the middle-of-the-night Venice streets, currently populated by dealers, hookers, and their pimps. She was too exhausted to care about any of them. Besides, her head and rib still throbbed after her altercation with Auggie.

As she approached Windward Circle, only blocks from where Ashley had gone missing, Keri's thoughts turned to Evie. How could she help some random teenage girl when she couldn't even help her own daughter?

Then it hit her—Evie was a teenage girl herself now. That is, if she was alive.

Shut up! Don't even think that. How dare you? She's counting on you to find her, to save her. If you give up, how is she supposed to stay strong? I will find you, Evie. I will! Don't give up, baby. Mommy hasn't. I love you so much.

She shook herself out of it. This was no use. She had to stay focused. When this case was over she'd approach Jackson Cave, find some way to *make* him tell her about the Collector. She wasn't just some college professor anymore. She had the full resources of the LAPD at her disposal and she intended to use them. She would find this Collector, or die trying.

And that was when she saw her, right there at the corner of Windward and Main. It was Evie!

She'd seen enough age-progression computer renderings to recognize the similarities. The blonde girl on the corner in the tight black miniskirt had the exact same bone structure and skin color as her daughter. Yes, she was heavily made up and forced to wear a slinky top that was offensive on a girl her age. But she was a match.

Keri almost retched at the sight of the large, pasty white man beside her, his hand firmly resting on the small of her back. He was well past forty and easily six feet tall and 250 pounds. And he was clearly her pimp.

Keri slammed her foot on the brakes. The Prius fishtailed to a stop near the curb they stood on. She hopped out and hurried around the car.

"Evie!" she shouted.

The large man stepped forward to block her way.

She tried to shove him aside to get to her girl but he grabbed her hard by the right wrist.

"What do you think you're doing, you crazy bitch?"

Keri didn't even look at him. Her eyes were focused solely on Evie.

"You're going to want to take your hands off me, Jabba," she growled.

He squeezed her wrist even harder.

"Even middle-aged females don't get to touch the merchandise before negotiating," he said.

Keri realized that with him holding her right wrist, her weapon was inaccessible. He was lucky. Otherwise she would have already shot him.

She stopped pulling and he involuntarily loosened his grip. She knew she couldn't break free but she'd gotten him to lower his guard. She moved toward him and stomped on the top of his foot with her heel. He grunted and bent over but didn't let go. She swung around and clocked his now lowered head with her left elbow. He let go and stumbled backward.

She would have reached for her gun but her wrist felt weak and numb. She wasn't sure she could hold it, much less shoot it. Instead, she stepped toward him and kicked, hoping to use his backward momentum to knock him to the ground. She made good contact but he managed to grab her ankle as he fell and brought her down with him.

No longer underestimating her, the pimp immediately rolled over so that his entire weight was on top of her. He pressed his knees into her already tender ribs, causing her to cry out in pain. He reached down and wrapped his arms around her neck. His eyes were bright with fury and spittle dripped from his mouth down into her hair.

Keri sensed she only had a few seconds of consciousness left. She glanced over at Evie, who was standing unmoving and horrified on the curb. Her vision started to blur.

I'm not going out like this!

Keri forced herself to focus on the man on top of her. He was strong but also overconfident.

Use that.

With one swift, deft motion, she raised both hands in unison and jabbed her thumbs in both his wide open eyes. He howled and let go of her immediately. She wasted no time in reaching back and using all her strength to punch him in the Adam's apple. He gagged and coughed. As he opened his mouth to gasp for air, she slammed his chin up with the open base of her palm. She heard him scream and knew his teeth had slammed shut on his tongue.

She pushed him off and rolled over before stumbling to her feet. Before he could regroup, she kicked him in the back and he fell to the ground, splayed out on his stomach. She dropped on top of him, jamming her knee in the small of his back. Pulling out her handcuffs with one hand, she grabbed one of his arms, cuffed his wrist, and then secured it to the other. She stood up again and placed her foot on the back of his neck.

"Don't move, asshole," she told him, "or you'll be using a colostomy bag for life."

His body went slack and she could tell he wasn't going to put up any more of a fight. She allowed herself a long, deep breath before she pulled out her radio and called for backup. Finally, she turned to face Evie, who was still standing petrified under a streetlight.

It was only then, in the harsh light and up close, that she realized it wasn't Evie at all. In fact, other than being young, blonde, and white, they didn't really look that much alike.

Keri could feel a sob rising to her throat and forced it back down. She looked down at her radio and pretended to mess with one of the dials so the girl in front of her couldn't see the devastation in her eyes. When she was sure she could speak without her voice breaking, she looked up again and spoke.

"What's your name, honey?"

"Sky."

"No, your real name."

"I'm not supposed to—"

"Tell me your real name."

The girl sized up the man on the ground, as if expecting him to jump up and grab her by the throat, and then said, "Susan."

"What's your last name, Susan?"

"Granger."

"Susan Granger?"

"Yes."

"How old are you, Susan?"

"Fourteen."

"Fourteen? Did you run away from home?"

The girl's eyes watered up.

"Yes."

"Well, me and some other people are going to help you," Keri said. "Would you like that?"

The girl hesitated and then said, "Yeah."

"You won't have to worry about this guy anymore," Keri said. "He's done hurting you. Has he been making you have sex with men?"

The girl nodded.

"Is he making you take drugs?"

"Uh-huh."

"Well, that's all over," Keri said. "We're going to get you somewhere safe, starting right now. Do you understand?"

"Yes."

"Good. Trust me, you're safe now."

Two black-and-whites pulled up.

"The officers in one of these cars are going to take you somewhere safe for the night. You'll meet with a counselor in the morning. I'm going to give you my card and I want you to use it if you have any questions. I'm searching for a missing girl about your age right now. But once I find her I'm going to check back in with you to make sure you're all right, okay, Susan?"

The girl nodded and took the card.

As the officers led her away, Keri leaned in close to the pimp, still splayed out on the ground, and whispered, "It's taking everything I have right now to keep from shooting you in the back of the head. Do you understand what I'm saying?"

The man twisted his neck, looked at her, and said, "Screw you."

Despite her fatigue, Keri's body vibrated with rage. She stepped away from him without responding for fear of doing exactly what she'd promised him. The uniformed officers came over. As one grabbed the perp to put him in the car, Keri spoke to the other.

"Book him. Make sure he doesn't get his phone call for at least a few hours. I don't want him making bail before we can safely place the girl. I'll be in to write my report after I get a few hours' sleep."

She saw the other officer about to guide the pimp's head down into the back seat of the car and stepped over.

"Let me help with that," she offered, grabbing the man by the hair and slamming the side of his head against the side of the roof. "Oh, sorry, I slipped."

She headed back to her car, the sound of his curses in the distance serving as sweet music.

As she drove home, finally headed to the houseboat, she dialed a number she rarely called.

"Hello," a sleepy female voice said.

"It's Keri Locke. I need to talk to you."

"Now? It's four in the morning."

"Yes."

A pause, and then, "Okay."

CHAPTER TWENTY ONE

Tuesday
Predawn

"I'm unraveling." She pictured the disappointment she knew must be on the face her department-ordered psychiatrist, Dr. Beverly Blanc.

"How so?"

Keri explained, letting it all spill out at once.

She was seeing Evie's face everywhere. She couldn't stop thinking about her. Maybe it was because the five-year mark was coming up next week. She didn't know. All she knew was that it was happening, more often than any time since the first six months after the abduction. She hadn't had any blank time in the last six months. But now she'd had multiple blank-out episodes in the last twelve hours. Worse, she'd gotten violent. She punched a high-school kid in the head. She'd swung a microphone into another guy's head. And she'd deliberately confronted both a drug dealer and a pimp.

She got a lead that Evie may have been taken by someone called the Collector. A local attorney, Jackson Cave, might know the man's real name and whereabouts but would never tell anyone voluntarily. Keri was entertaining thoughts of blackmailing him to force him to talk.

Also, she was working the Ashley Penn case.

"I know," Dr. Blanc said. "I saw you on TV."

She was on the case, then got kicked off it, then got back on it; right now, she didn't know what her status was.

Dr. Blanc said, "You have more coming in than you can process. You're like a balloon with too much air pumping into it. If it doesn't stop, you're going to explode. You need to either get off the Ashley Penn case or put Evie on hold. Stop thinking about her until this case is resolved."

Keri winced.

"I can't drop the case."

"Why not?"

"Because if I do, and something ends up happening, I couldn't live with myself."

Dr. Blanc exhaled.

"Then you have to let Evie go for now. You have to stop fixating on her. And you have to do the same with the Collector."

"That's impossible."

"Look," Dr. Blanc said, "here's the reality. If Evie's dead—"

"She's not!"

"Okay, but *if* she is, setting thoughts of her aside for a while is not going to affect her one way or the other. If she's *not* dead, then she's probably found a way to cope with her current life. The fear and desperation that you saw on her face the last time you saw her, it's not there right now."

"We don't know that," Keri said.

"Yes, we do," Dr. Blanc said. "Emotions like that are not sustainable. If she's alive, wherever she is, the overwhelming chances are that she's found a way to function day to day. She's in some kind of a routine. She's adjusted to it. Setting the Collector and this lawyer guy to the side for a week or two is not going to make a significant difference to Evie in the grand scheme of her life.

"In fact, if you rush into hunting down this Collector guy, you might even make mistakes that you wouldn't make later when you're thinking straight. You might tip him off that you're coming. He might slip away. So, clear him from your mind, the lawyer too, and work the Ashley Penn case if that's what you have to do, then go back at him when you're healthy and you can give him your full concentration. Does that make sense?"

Keri exhaled. "Yes."

"You need rest, too, Keri. Rest is extremely important. Go home and sleep at least eight hours. Consider that the doctor's orders."

"I can maybe try for three."

"I'll take it."

*

Keri went home.

These days, home was a deteriorating twenty-year-old houseboat slipped at Marina Bay in Marina del Rey. There was a fancy part of the marina further west, with expensive apartment buildings and yacht clubs. But Basin H, where Keri lived, was much more working class. Her place was housed among industrial fishing boats and the barely seaworthy vessels of old-timers. The prior owner had named it *Sea Cups*, and hand-painted a pink bra on the side. It wasn't exactly Keri's style but she'd never worked up the time or energy to scrape it off.

The good news was that it had electricity, water, a small galley, and a pump-out toilet, and it didn't tie her down. She could abandon it without a second thought and run off to Alaska if her life suddenly demanded it. The bad news was that it had no shower or laundry. Those tasks needed to be done down the road at the Marina's comfort station, or at work.

It also had almost no room to spare. Everything was in something else's way. If you wanted one thing, you had to move three. For people with houses, the thought of living in a houseboat might seem adventurous or exotic. For someone like Keri, who actually did it every day, the charm had long since worn off.

Keri went to the galley, poured herself a generous serving of scotch, and headed for the roof deck. As she got to the stairwell, she saw that a framed photo had tipped over. The houseboat didn't rock much but on occasion it moved enough to cause things to shift or fall over. She righted the photo, glancing at it without really processing what she was seeing.

After a moment, she realized she was staring at what used to be her family. It was one of those posed beach photos they'd done as part of Evie's preschool fundraiser when she was four. They sat by a section of rocks with the ocean in the background. Evie was in front in a white sundress. Her blonde hair was kept out of her eyes by a green headband that matched her eyes.

Both parents sat behind her. Stephen had on khaki slacks and an untucked white dress shirt. Keri was dressed similarly in a flowing white blouse and a khaki skirt. Stephen had one hand on Evie's shoulder and the other wrapped around Keri's waist. That remnant of their casual intimacy flashed through her mind. It had been a long time since anyone had touched her in that comfortable, knowing way.

She remembered that it had been hard not to squint that day because the photo sitting was in the morning and the bright early fall sun was right in their eyes. Evie kept complaining about it but somehow managed to open her eyes wide for this one shot. Keri couldn't help but smile at the memory.

She left the picture behind as she walked up the stairs to the deck and settled into a cheap chaise lounge she'd ordered from Amazon on impulse. She closed her eyes and tried to feel the nearly imperceptible movement of the houseboat. The photo drifted through her mind again. The Keri Locke in that picture wouldn't recognize her now.

It had been taken almost four years before Evie was abducted. Looking back, that was about as close to perfect as Keri's life had ever been. She'd somehow survived a childhood she wouldn't wish on anyone to become a successful professor of criminology and psychology at LMU. She was a respected consultant for the LAPD. She was married to a prominent entertainment attorney who never let his work interfere with a preschool recital or Halloween parade.

And she had a daughter who made her see every day that growing up didn't have to be about trauma. It could be about wonder and joy. There were pumpkin patches to visit and chocolate chip cookies to bake together. There were furtive, hurried Sunday morning lovemaking sessions to enjoy before little feet could be heard galloping into their bedroom. Those were the salad days and she hadn't even realized it.

The Keri of the past would be aghast at the current one, gulping liquor like it was water, alone on a houseboat named after a bra size. She tried to reconstruct how it had all fallen apart. First came the drinking to oblivion, then the screaming matches with a husband who had become distant and cold. Keri knew now that it had been a form of self-protection, a way for Stephen to survive the living nightmare they shared, to keep it at arm's length. But at the time it had infuriated her, made her think he didn't care what had happened to their daughter.

After he finally left her a year later and moved out, their house felt somehow both empty and too full of memories, so she moved onto the houseboat. She also moved from guy to guy at the university. Sometimes it was grad students, sometimes undergrads—whoever was willing to make her feel good for a few moments and help her forget the anguish that consumed most of her waking hours.

That went on for about a year, until one particularly naïve, love-struck nineteen-year-old dropped out of school because Keri had casually moved on. His parents threatened to sue. The historically Jesuit school had no choice but to settle quickly and quietly. Part of the agreement was that Keri be fired.

It was around that time that Stephen told her that he was marrying one of his clients, a young actress with sixth billing on a medical drama. They were having a baby, a little boy. Keri had gone on a week-long bender at that news. It was soon after that when a former colleague, a detective from Pacific Division named Ray Sands, had come by the boat with a proposal.

"I hear things haven't gone your way lately," he said, sitting on the same deck Keri was curled up on now. "Maybe you need a new start."

He told her about his own trip down the rabbit hole of despair and how he'd managed to crawl out by choosing to stop feeling sorry for himself and make a difference with what life he still had.

"Have you ever thought about applying to the Police Academy?" he'd asked.

The marina was quiet now, save for the sound of waves lapping up onto boat hulls and a distant foghorn calling mournfully into the darkness. Keri could feel herself drifting and chose not to fight it. She put down her glass, pulled a blanket over her, and closed her eyes.

*

Her reverie was interrupted by the ringing of her cell phone. She looked at the screen, blinking away the blurriness. It was 5:45. She'd been asleep for less than two hours. She squinted to see who was calling. It was Ray. She picked up.

"I was finally sleeping," she said irritably.

"They found the black van!"

CHAPTER TWENTY TWO

Tuesday
Dawn

Powered mostly by adrenaline, Keri got off the 210 Freeway near La Canada-Flintridge and headed north on the Angeles Crest Highway. The sun was rising on her right and she could see the Jet Propulsion Laboratory in the distance as she followed the winding two-lane road into the Angeles National Forest.

Within minutes, the huge city just to the south was forgotten and she was surrounded by towering trees as she made her way up the side of a steep, craggy mountain. At a little after 6:30 she reached her destination, a rest station and bathroom on a small dirt road just west of Woodwardia Canyon.

Down a quarter of a mile, four police vehicles faced a black van. Two were LAPD and two more were LA County Sheriff. A CSU truck was there too and she could see investigators poring over the vehicle, collecting evidence. Ray and Hillman were off to the side of the road, talking. Detectives Sterling and Cantwell were there too, listening intently.

Keri got out and headed over. She wished she'd remembered a jacket. At this hour in the mountains it was chilly, even during a heat wave. She shivered slightly, unsure whether it was the cold or the sight in front of her.

The van's doors were all open. Inside, there was no blood or signs of a struggle. The ashtray was full of butts. In the back, a brown bag full of granola bars, chips, Gatorade, and crackers had split open. The keys were in the ignition.

Ray saw Keri and walked over.

"They were running away," he said, showing her a handwritten note inside a clear evidence bag.

> *I'm going to start a new life.*
> *All I want is for everyone to leave me alone.*
> *If you bring me back I'll just run away again.*
> *Ashley*

Keri shook her head.

"This is bullshit."

"No, it's legit," Ray said. "We took a photo of it and texted it to Mia Penn. She says that's definitely Ashley's handwriting. Also,

119

the piece of paper is stationery that Ashley got for her birthday. The note was pinned to the dash with an earring, which was also definitely Ashley's."

"I don't buy it," Keri said.

"Look around, Keri," Ray said. "You're on the Angeles Crest Highway headed northeast. My guess is they planned to avoid the authorities by staying on it until about Wrightwood, then hook up with the Fifteen Freeway north to Vegas. From what we can tell, they stopped here to use the facilities. When they got back to the van, it wouldn't start."

"How do you know?"

"We tried, watch." He led her over, adjusted his gloves, and cranked the key. Nothing happened. "The battery terminal is caked with corrosion. The battery's not making contact with the cable."

"Hell, all you have to do is work it off and scrape the inside with a key and then twist it back on."

"You know that, I know that, but a fifteen-year-old girl doesn't know that," he said. "It didn't start and they hitched their way out of here."

"You keep saying 'they.' Who was she with?" she asked.

"God only knows with this girl."

Keri stood quietly, trying to make sense of it.

Then she said, "Who does the van belong to?"

"Dexter Long."

Keri had never heard the name before.

"Who's he?"

"He's a college kid at Occidental College," Ray said. "The van is registered to him. Someone apparently stole it from a campus garage. The kid didn't even know it was gone. He lives in a dorm and hasn't even driven it in over a month."

"He didn't lend it to anybody?"

"No."

"Then how did someone get the keys?"

"He leaves them up in the visor."

"With the door unlocked?"

"Apparently so."

"Shit."

"Yeah."

"So, are you getting prints?"

"They already did," Ray said. "But if she's with another teenager who's not old enough to drive, unless the kid's got a record, they won't have anything to match them to."

Hillman came over and said, "We've been spinning our wheels for nothing."

Keri frowned.

"You think it's legit? That Ashley ran away?"

He nodded.

"There's nothing else to think," he said. "I don't know with who, or why, exactly, but I don't really care at this point. As far as I'm concerned, it's no longer an LAPD case."

"What do you mean?"

"It's no longer in our jurisdiction. County has offered to coordinate with the FBI when they officially take over," Hillman said. "We're all going back to cases where people are actually missing. There's no shortage of them."

"But—"

Hillman cut her off.

"No buts," he said. "We're off the case. Don't defy me on this, Locke. You're on thin ice as it is. By my count you've been in physical altercations with at least three people in just the last twelve hours. And that's only the ones I know about. All this renegade stuff, it's going to stop. I'm trying to make this as clear as I can because I'm deadly serious."

Ray put a hand on Keri's shoulder.

"I think Lieutenant Hillman may have a point on this one," he said. "We pursued every lead. But nothing definitively shows that Ashley Penn was even abducted, Keri. Meanwhile, we have lots of stuff that suggests she ran away."

"That could have been planted."

"Anything's possible, I guess. But if so, County and FBI will determine that. Let it go, Keri. Ashley Penn isn't your daughter. She's a troubled girl but she isn't our problem anymore."

"If you're wrong, then we're wasting valuable time."

"I'll take the heat for that," Hillman said before walking off.

Yeah, but you're not the one who will be having nightmares.

CHAPTER TWENTY THREE

Tuesday
Dawn

When Ashley woke up, she could tell right away that something was different. The inside of the silo was no longer pitch-black. Rather, faint rays of sunlight squeezed in at the edges of the hatch at the top. It was enough to allow her to make out things without using the flashlight.

She bolted upright. After taking a moment to adjust, she noticed something else.

A beam of daylight was also squirting through a hole in the wall of the silo. The hole was the size of a quarter, up the wall a bit above her head. When she jumped up, she could almost get an eye to it but not quite.

She needed a stepstool. Rifling through the bin of food, she found some of the soup cans. She stacked them on the floor on either side of the hole and then laid the loose board across them, creating a plank. Gingerly climbing up and resting her hands on the inner wall of the silo, she was able to get an eye to the hole and look out. She saw an old dilapidated barn, a small farmhouse, and rutted dirt roads running through the fields that were long since abandoned and now choked with weeds. Rusty hulks of abandoned cars and distressed farm machinery littered the grounds.

Looking down, she got a sense of how high she was. The silo was easily forty feet tall.

She didn't like heights and never had. She didn't even like the high diving board at the pool.

There were no signs of life outside—no people, no cars, no dogs, nothing. Her abductor was nowhere to be found.

Taking another look down the chute, she spied a fair amount of light down below, almost as if it were coming through a door or window at the base of the silo. She hung the board straight down and jammed the end against the bones until they dropped through. With the chute now open, she could see to the bottom. It looked like a dirt floor below with a small pile of old grain. Based on how deep the bones had settled into the grain, she guessed it was two to three inches thick.

Could I drop down?

Taking another look down, she pictured the fall. It was a long way. She doubted the thin layer of grain would offer much of a cushion. And the chute—was it big enough for her to get through? It would be close. What would be the best position for her body? With her arms straight down at her sides or pointed up above her head? She pictured getting stuck with arms down and then with her arms up. What would be her preferred position if she was wedged in that hole for the rest of her life? She shook the thought from her mind.

Not constructive.

Right now, with only one board removed, she couldn't drop down even if she wanted to. She'd have to remove another board. She debated her options.

Screw it. I'm doing this.

She could at least get another board out and have the option available.

Ashley was more efficient this time, getting the board removed in two hours. Then she had an idea. Using the pull-off top from a can of soup, she cut the mattress apart and then wedged the foam padding and the outer cotton pieces down through the chute to the ground below. They all landed in the same general area, creating an additional six to eight inches of support. If she landed right on top of the pile, she might have as much as ten inches of cushion. It wasn't much from that height but it was better than before. Plus, the padding covered most of the bones, so at least the chances of one of them jamming into her on impact were reduced. It was the little things.

She looked at the bin of food, wondering if she should toss some of it down to take with her. It was an intriguing option. But she worried that doing so might mess up the padding or that something hard might get stuck in it. No point in doing all this hard work just to land on a soup can and break her back.

Then a thought occurred to her that made her so proud she actually smiled for the first time since this nightmare started. She pulled off her skirt and top and tossed them down the chute as well. Now wearing only her bra and panties, she grabbed the peanut butter from the bin.

She might be allergic to the stuff but maybe it could come in handy in another way. She opened it and began slathering the goop all over her body, paying extra attention to her outer thighs, butt, hips, stomach, and rib cage. When she dropped with her arms over her head, maybe being coated in the slick substance would help her get through the chute.

When she was done, Ashley allowed herself a moment to focus quietly. She could feel herself starting to get herself psyched for the drop, like she would before a big surfing competition. Almost involuntarily, her breathing slowed. Everything seemed sharper. It was time.

She stepped to the edge and looked down.

Although she was in the right position, she didn't like the idea of dropping into the chute from a standing position. There'd be less of a fall if she got in the hole, hung from one of the remaining boards and then let go. She positioned the flashlight to point into the chute so she'd have a good visual when she dropped. Then she climbed over the edge of the flooring and hung down, dangling above the chute.

Okay, do it! Goodbye, Mom. Goodbye, Daddy! I love you both. I'm sorry about everything.

I don't want to die.

Her breathing got rapid; in and out, in and out.

She could feel herself freaking out.

No! This is crazy!

She tried frantically to get back up but couldn't. The strength in her arms just wasn't there anymore.

She was stuck with no choice but to drop.

At that realization, her breath slowed again. The inevitability gave her an unexpected feeling of calmness. She closed her eyes for a long second and opened them again, ready to focus on her task. She swayed back and forth slightly so that she could drop directly over the chute opening at the ideal time.

When the moment was right, Ashley Penn released her grip and dropped into a freefall.

CHAPTER TWENTY FOUR

Tuesday
Early Morning

Keri racked her brain all the way back to Venice. Everything pointed to Ashley having run away, just as Hillman and Ray believed. Factually, it fit all the evidence. Still, it didn't feel right. Back in the city, she didn't go to the station. She didn't want to deal with the condescending looks and hushed whispers she knew would be waiting for her there.

Instead, she drove aimlessly by all the spots she rushed to last night—Ashley's school, the Blue Mist Lounge, through the art district where Walker Lee lived, anywhere familiar. An hour into it, she called Mia Penn and said, "Do you believe that Ashley ran away?"

"I don't want to. But I have to admit it's possible."

"Seriously?"

"Look, based on everything I've learned in the last day, it's pretty obvious that I had no idea who my own daughter was," she said. "How does something like that even happen?"

"Kids hide things," Keri said.

"Yeah, I know, but this was like…I don't know, so extreme, all the things she was doing. I thought I had a good relationship with her. In the end, though, it's like she didn't trust me enough to tell me anything. I've been trying to figure out what I did to alienate her…"

"Don't blame yourself," Keri said. "I've been there. I'm still there. I don't wish it on anyone."

"Look," Mia said. "I'm choosing to believe that Ashley left on her own. She'll call us sooner or later and we'll find out what we did wrong. I'm prepared to wait and give her space."

"I can come over—"

"No."

"But—"

"It's not a good idea," Mia said. "Between you and me, Stafford's gone into a rage over that Amber Alert. He trashed our bedroom this morning. He thinks he's going to lose his Senate seat over all the negative publicity, he's convinced of it."

"He blames me?" Keri said.

"Just stay away. It'll pass, but for now, keep your distance."

"We could review the evidence," Keri said.

"Keri, nothing personal, but stop!"

The connection died.

Up the road, in a school zone, a black van was abruptly pulling away. Keri saw movement in the back window, what looked like blonde hair bouncing up and down.

Ashley floored it and managed to get alongside. The driver was a pockmarked man in his mid-thirties with long greasy brown hair and a cigarette dangling from the hand resting on the window. Keri motioned for him to pull over. He gave her the finger and sped up.

She pursued him, reaching over to put the siren on her roof. Just as she was about to turn it on, the light ahead of them turned red and the van screeched to a halt. Keri swerved to the right to avoid ramming him from behind. She hit the brakes hard and threw the car into park. Stepping out of the Prius, she held up her badge for the man to see through the open passenger side window.

"When I give you an order to pull over, you comply!"

The man nodded.

"Now get out of the goddamn car and walk around to this side."

The man complied.

Keeping him in one eye, Keri swung open the side door of the van. No one was inside. There were flowers, nothing else. She glanced at the sliding door and noticed something she'd missed before: a sign reading *Brandy's Floral Delivery*.

The man had come around the front of the vehicle and was standing in front of her.

"Open the back door," she demanded.

He did. There were no children inside. Just more flowers. She realized that what she thought was blonde hair was most likely a bunch of sunflowers at the very back of the van.

I am completely losing it.

Keri looked at the driver and could tell he was deciding whether he should be confused, scared, or angry. She decided she had better make the choice for him.

"Listen to me," she growled. "You pulled out of that side street like a bat out of hell in the middle of a school zone. And then, when I order you to pull over, you flick me off? You're lucky I don't bring you in just on general principal."

"I'm sorry about pulling out like that. But I didn't know you were a cop. Some lady in a Prius with a crazy look in her eyes wants me to pull over, I'm not automatically gonna do it. You gotta see it from my side."

"That's the only reason I'm letting you go with a warning. I was this close to ramming your ass. Drive slow—got it?"

"Yes ma'am."

"Good. Now get out of here."

He did as he was told. Keri returned to her car and just sat in it for a minute, contemplating how close she'd come to assaulting another random person. And this wasn't a drug dealer or a pimp or even a preening wannabe rock star. It was just a flower delivery guy. She needed to reel it in but couldn't seem to figure out how. She still had an itch she needed to scratch. And until she'd gotten satisfaction, she knew she'd never be able to calm down.

The moment she realized that, Keri knew there was only one place to go and it wasn't home or the station. In fact, it was less than a five-minute drive from her current location.

*

As Keri parked her car on the narrow residential street overrun with news vans, reporters, paparazzi, and rubberneckers, she finished up her call. She'd been talking to the Child Protective Services officer assigned to Susan Granger's case. The woman, Margaret Rondo, assured her that Susan would be sent to a secure women and children's shelter. It was in Redondo Beach on a neighborhood street and looked like any other house from the outside, except that the exterior walls were a little high and there were a few unobtrusively placed cameras. Susan's pimp, whom Keri had learned went by the name Crabby, would never be able to find her.

And thanks to Detective Suarez, Crabby's paperwork had mysteriously been misplaced and he'd be stuck down at the Twin Towers facility for another forty-eight hours, more than enough time for Keri to write a report that would ensure he didn't get a reasonable bail.

After some prodding, Rondo reluctantly let Keri speak to Susan briefly.

"How are you doing?" she asked.

"Scared. I thought you would be here."

"I'm still looking for that missing girl I told you about. But when everything settles down, I promise to check in on you, okay?"

"Uh-huh." Susan sounded deflated.

"Susan—I bet a lot of people have made you promises and broken them, haven't they?"

"Yes."

"And I can tell you think I'm going to do the same thing, right?"

"Maybe."

"Well, I'm not a lot of people. Have you ever seen anyone take care of Crabby like I did last night?"

"No."

"Do you think someone like that, who had a huge, smelly guy on top of him and ended up with him on his stomach in cuffs, do you think someone who did that can't find her way to visit you?"

"I guess not."

"Damn straight, forgive my language. I will be there when I can. And when I get there, I'll show you some of the moves I used. Sound good?"

"Yeah. Can you show me the thumb in the eyes thing?"

"Of course. But we only use that one in emergencies, okay?"

"I've been in a lot of emergencies."

"I know you have, sweetie," Keri said, refusing to let her voice crack. "But that's all over now. See you soon, okay?"

"Okay."

Keri hung up and sat quietly in the car for a moment. She allowed herself to imagine all the horrors Susan Granger had been through, but only for a few seconds. And when she felt thoughts of Evie in the same situation sneaking into her brain, she pushed them away. This wasn't the time for wallowing. This was a time for action.

She got out of the car and walked briskly toward the Penn residence. It was almost eight in the morning—late enough for a house call. Truthfully, she didn't care what time it was. Something about her most recent phone conversation with Mia didn't sit right. It had been eating at her ever since. And she was about to get some answers.

The second she was spotted, a swarm of reporters surrounded her. She didn't break stride and a few of them tripped over each other trying to keep up with her. She fought the smile at the corner of her lips. Once she passed through the mansion's gate, the reporters stopped, as if there were some sort of force field preventing them from going any further.

She banged on the door. The security guard from her first visit opened it. When she barreled past him into the house, he hesitated, obviously briefly considering stopping her. But one look in her eyes and he stopped himself.

"They're in the kitchen," he said. "Please let me lead the way. If you just storm in, they'll think I'm useless and fire me."

Keri did him that courtesy and slowed enough to let him take the lead. When they entered the kitchen, Keri saw Mia sitting at the breakfast table in her bathrobe, weakly sipping some coffee.

Stafford Penn's back was to her as he flipped from channel to channel on the kitchen television. Every station was covering Ashley.

Mia looked up and the tired expression on her face vanished. Her eyes flashed with—not anger—something closer to fear. She started to speak.

"I thought I told you—"

Keri held up her hand, and something about her bearing made Mia stop mid-sentence. Senator Penn turned around to see what the commotion was. He opened his mouth, but seeing the look on Keri's face, he too stopped himself.

"First off, you should know that I'm going to be dispensing with the polite formalities. One, there isn't time for it. And two, I don't have the patience."

"What are you talking about?" Senator Penn demanded.

Keri focused on Mia.

"I know you don't think Ashley ran away any more than I do. All yesterday and into the night, you pushed for us to investigate. You were certain she was abducted. Then I call you this morning and suddenly you think she left on her own? You want to give her space? I don't buy it. Not for a second."

"Frankly, I don't care what you believe," Stafford Penn said. "I told you all along that this was a teenage girl sowing her oats. And now it turns out I was right. You just don't want to look bad."

Keri studied him closely. The man was a politician, clearly a successful one to reach his current position. And he was adept at making people believe him, whether it be constituents or reporters or teenage girls he knocked up in his law office.

But Keri wasn't any of those. She was a detective with the LAPD. And she was pretty good at spotting a liar, even one as practiced as Senator Stafford Penn.

"You're lying to me. And so help me God, I don't care if you're a senator or the president of the United States, I don't care if it costs me my job. I will take you in for impeding an investigation. And I'll do it by walking you out those doors in cuffs in front of all those reporters and tossing you in the back seat of my tiny, dented hatchback. Let's see you get reelected after that."

Out of the corner of her eye Keri saw the security guard cover his mouth to hide his wide grin.

"What do you want?" Penn hissed through gritted teeth.

I want to know the exact thing you're hiding from me.

Stafford didn't hesitate, "I'm not hiding anything."

Mia looked at him. "Stafford—"

"Mia, stop."

"Come on, Stafford, enough already."

"We're done here," the senator said, staring at Keri. She stared back for several seconds.

"Apparently we are," she agreed, pulling out her cuffs and stepping toward him.

Mia stood up.

"Tell her," she said in a forceful tone Keri had never heard from her before.

He shook his head.

"She has no right."

"Stafford, tell her or I will."

He exhaled, then shook his head as if astonished at the stupidity of what he was about to do.

"Wait here." He headed upstairs. A minute later he came back down and handed Keri a piece of paper. "This was in our mailbox this morning." The paper was plain white and the words were typed.

You have wronged me. Now you will be wronged.
Payback is a bitch. Prepare to face the music.

"I can't believe you were sitting on this," Keri said.

Stafford sighed. "It's not legit."

"Why do you say that?"

"Because I'm ninety percent sure who sent it."

"Who?"

"Payton Penn; he's my half-brother," Stafford said. "We have the same father, different mothers."

Keri said, "I still don't get it."

"Payton, to put it mildly, is a loser," Stafford said. "He hates this family. He hates me, because of some events that occurred when we were growing up. Plus, he's obviously jealous of how my life turned out. He hates Mia, because he could never get someone like her. And he hates Ashley, mostly because Ashley hates him. He knows stuff about our family, including something the public doesn't know and which I'm sharing with you in confidence: I'm Ashley's real father."

Keri nodded solemnly, pretending to be flattered and surprised by his big reveal.

"I appreciate you trusting me with that information, Senator. I know your privacy is important to you and I won't violate that. But I'm waiting for the part where you explain why your half-brother shouldn't be a suspect."

"We've been paying him hush money ever since I became a senator to keep quiet about Ashley and…a few other things we don't need to go into now. So it makes no sense for him to rock the boat now. He's putting his guaranteed money at risk. Plus it's not even really a ransom note."

"What do you mean?"

"It's typical Payton. He's not willing to go all the way. Look how vague the letter is. 'You have wronged me'? That could be from thousands of people here or in Washington. He never even actually asks for money."

"So what do *you* think is going on?"

"Knowing my brother, he heard about Ashley being missing and thought he could capitalize on it by writing this letter. But he didn't have the balls to actually demand a ransom. He just sort of left the option open for the future if he was able to screw up his courage. It's either that or he figured this was a good time to twist the knife in, when I'm at my lowest point. He doesn't get many chances to stick it to me. So he didn't want to waste this one."

"Okay. But what makes you so confident that he didn't discover his balls and actually take her?"

"Because when Ashley went missing yesterday after school and Mia started flipping out, I called a private investigator I use occasionally, just to check on him. Payton was at work all day yesterday until five. As you know, Ashley got into the van a little after three."

"Are you positive he was at work?"

"Yes. The investigator sent me a copy of the building's surveillance footage. He's all over it."

"He could have hired someone."

"He doesn't have the money for that."

"I thought you were paying him."

"Not enough to hire someone to steal my daughter."

"Maybe his partner is planning on getting a windfall from the ransom."

"The ransom he hasn't asked for? Enough, Detective. I've answered your questions. This is a dead-end. And just so you know, I'm calling Lieutenant Hillman to report that you threatened me. With your service record, I'm not sure how well that will go for you."

"Oh, shut up, Stafford!" Mia yelled at him. "If you cared half as much about your daughter as your career, none of this would be happening!"

He looked like he'd been slapped in the face. His eyes rimmed slightly with tears and he turned away quickly without responding, focusing his attention back on the television.

"I'll walk you out," Mia said. As they headed for the front door, a thought occurred to Keri.

"Mia, did Payton ever have access to the house?"

"Well, we tried to reconcile with him a few times over the years. We even let him stay with us for the long weekend last Easter. It didn't go well."

"Was he always supervised?"

"No, I mean, that would have defeated the point. We were trying to resolve all these issues. Having security tail him all weekend would have undermined that trust a little, don't you think?"

"And it ended badly?"

"He and Stafford got into a screaming match and he left early. That's the last time we saw him."

"Thank you," Keri said and quickly left. The press was still outside and she didn't want to look suspicious so she tried not to sprint to her car.

But she came close.

There was something she needed to do urgently.

CHAPTER TWENTY FIVE

Tuesday
Mid-morning

As Keri sped up the winding roads of Highway 18 toward Lake Arrowhead, her phone rang. She'd hoped that up here in the mountains she wouldn't have a connection and it would go straight to voicemail. No such luck. Against her better judgment, she picked up, hitting the speaker button on the console.

Lieutenant Hillman's voice came through loud and clear.

"Where are you?" he demanded. He wasn't yelling but she could tell it was taking all his effort.

"I'm going to Payton Penn's cabin up at Lake Arrowhead."

"Turn around now," he said. "I told you before that the County and the FBI were taking over the case. Instead of following my orders, you decide to harass a US senator?"

"I wasn't harassing. I was investigating."

"Keri—" He sounded almost pleading.

"Stafford has a half-brother, Payton Penn, who put a note in his mailbox."

"I already know that," Hillman said.

"You do?"

"Yes," he said. "And we're checking him out. But so far what the senator said seems to bear out. Everything supports the theory that she ran away. At most, this is an amateurish attempt to take advantage of the situation to extort money. Penn doesn't want to pursue it criminally. It's a family issue that he wants to handle quietly."

"We should at least check it out."

"The Feds are. And if anything turns up, they'll pursue it. But you going out there only draws attention to something Penn wants to keep quiet."

"Do we work for him now?" she asked, more forcefully than she'd intended.

"Detective, stop!" Hillman shouted. "I want you to turn around right now. You are officially off this case."

"Look, I'm almost to Payton's. I'll just check around to confirm that Ashley's not there. I'll be in and out in five minutes."

"Detective Locke," he said in a calm, quiet voice that worried her more than when he yelled, "you are an enormously skilled cop. But your insubordination is unacceptable. I'm suspending you from

133

active duty, effective immediately. Return to the station and turn in your gun and your badge. You'll continue to receive pay pending a formal hearing, if you want one. But as of this moment, you are no longer authorized to act as a member of the Los Angeles Police Department. Do you understand me?"

Keri weighed his words, well aware that this was a point of no return. But she'd had many of those in the past. This was far from the worst. She spoke.

"Lieutenant Hillman, are you there?"

"Detective..." he growled.

"Lieutenant, are you there? Hello, hello? I think I'm losing you. You keep cutting out."

"Locke, don't you dare pretend—"

Keri ended the call.

*

Keri parked about a quarter mile down the road from Payton Penn's cabin, deep in the San Bernardino Mountains. She got out slowly, taken aback by the quiet, the isolation. She felt that familiar knot in her stomach as she braced herself for what she might find as she went the rest of the way on foot.

When she reached his driveway, she discovered it was essentially a wide dirt path, leading up a steep hill into the trees. She couldn't even see the cabin from the road.

As she started up the incline, Keri wondered for the third time in the last hour if she should call Ray. They hadn't spoken since he'd embraced Hillman's theory about Ashley running away back at the van. She knew she shouldn't let her anger get in the way at a time like this. Sneaking onto a potentially dangerous suspect's property was a dicey proposition under any circumstances.

But alone was worse.

Ultimately she told herself that she was protecting him by not calling. Hillman had already suspended her. What would he do to Ray if he helped her? Part of her knew she was kidding herself. Ray would come if she asked, no matter what.

She shook the thought from her head. It was too late for that. She was on her own. And she needed to stay on her toes.

The scent of pine wafted through the air as she ascended higher. Her breathing was labored. She felt sweat trickle down her back. Keri lived on a houseboat in a marina—the very definition of sea level. The elevation here was closer to 6,000 feet. And the cool morning was starting to give way to the late summer heat. She guessed it was already pushing eighty degrees. And her aches and pains from the run-ins with Johnnie Cotton and Crabby the pimp weren't helping. Walking was a struggle.

Suddenly a loud bang pierced the air—gunfire from up above. Apparently Payton Penn was home and he was armed.

Keri confirmed her weapon status and checked her cell phone reception. It was still surprisingly strong. She pressed on, fully aware that she was now technically a civilian with a gun on a private citizen's property. She was trespassing. Payton Penn could shoot her and make a reasonable case for self-defense.

For a fraction of a second, Keri considered turning back. This was not the wisest course of action. But if she didn't go up, she wasn't sure when, or if, anyone else would. How would she feel if she found out later that she was this close to Ashley and didn't take the last few steps to get to her?

Keri walked up dirt path, one careful step at a time, mindful of nearby boulders and trees in case she needed to duck for cover. She was closer to the gunfire now. It was intermittent, consistent with target practice.

She was far enough up the driveway that she could no longer hear traffic from the road below. Apart from the echoes from the gunfire, it was quiet up here. The tall trees muffled the noise and blocked out the sun. It felt more like dusk than the actual time— 9:45 AM. The road snaked up the side of the mountain, leading to the isolated cabin. Keri realized that this far up, no one would likely be able to hear anyone's screams for help.

It took another ten minutes of walking before the cabin came into sight. The decrepit old place stood in a large clearing in the middle of a circle of trees. An old pickup truck was parked near the front door. The gunfire, coming from behind the cabin, was now almost at full volume.

Keri ducked behind a moss-covered boulder and scoped the place out. No one came into view. The gunfire continued. If this was target practice, it was a long session. The guy was clearly enjoying himself. Keri wondered how he'd react if he spotted her, both of them with weapons in hand.

Her heart pounded. Sweat rolled down her forehead and into her eyes. She wiped at it with the back of her hand, steadied her breathing, surveyed the area one last time, and headed rapidly for the cabin. If Payton suddenly appeared around the corner, Keri would be in plain view.

The gunfire stopped.

Is he reloading? Is he done and heading back into the cabin?

She got to the pickup and squatted behind it, listening. Somewhere up above, a jet rumbled. To her right, bees worked on a patch of wild cactus, buzzing lightly as they flew from one set of needles to the next.

Keri stepped out from behind the pickup, stood there in the open for a heartbeat, and then quietly made her way to the side of the cabin, where she peeked through the screen door. The place was pretty much what she expected—a bulky couch, a ratty wooden coffee table with a dusty old laptop on it, a wood-burning stove, a sink filled with dirty dishes, clutter everywhere. Cigarette smoke hung in the air.

There was no sign of Ashley.

Suddenly the back door of the cabin opened and someone entered, not yet visible. Seconds later, he entered the main room. He bore a striking resemblance to Stafford but he looked harder, more weathered. He was unshaven and his eyes were bloodshot. Life had been tougher on him than Stafford. He wore dirty jeans and a loud red T-shirt. Sweat soaked through it at the armpits. He set two handguns on the coffee table. Then he went to the fridge, got a beer, and popped the top.

Keri decided that was as good a time as any to make her entrance. She pushed the unlocked screen door open and stepped inside.

"Don't move!" she yelled, her weapon pointed at his chest. They were only six feet apart.

Payton Penn did as he was ordered. The beer was at his lips and he made no move to bring it down. He seemed surprisingly calm, considering the circumstances.

"Where's Ashley Penn?" Keri demanded.

The man smiled.

"Is it okay if I put this beer down? You said don't move and I don't want to break the rules."

Keri nodded. He pulled the bottle away from his lips and reached out to put it on the end table. But at the last second he flicked it in her direction and leapt at her.

Keri had been prepared for something from him and sidestepped the bottle. She felt some beer splash on her neck but otherwise avoided contact entirely. Payton seemed to realize he had underestimated her but it was too late. She was no longer directly in his path and he couldn't stop his momentum.

Keri took her finger off the trigger and lifted the grip upward so that Payton's head slammed into the magazine butt plate. His legs wobbled and he fell to the ground, conscious but stunned.

"Get up," Keri ordered, tossing her handcuffs at him. "And put those on. If you try anything else, I'll shoot you in the kneecap."

He stumbled to his feet.

"Well, that was interesting," he said, smiling, and added, "Are you afraid to shoot me somewhere permanent?"

She pointed the weapon at his chest and narrowed her eyes.

"If you don't tell me where Ashley is, you're not much use to me. I may have to take you out back and use *you* for target practice."

Part of her hoped he'd come at her. The idea of making him bleed and cry was extremely appealing. But that wouldn't help Ashley. He seemed to sense that she was on the edge and put the cuffs on without argument. Then he seemed to regain his courage and looked her at her directly. His eyes were twinkling. Keri realized at that moment that he was half crazy.

"Apart from requesting my lawyer, I'd like to invoke my right to remain silent," he said before adding with a wink, "Now what?"

CHAPTER TWENTY SIX

Tuesday
Late Morning

Keri did a cursory pat-down of Penn before cuffing him to the radiator. Then she searched the property, calling out Ashley's name. She opened as many doors and banged on as many walls as she could without messing things up too much for CSU. When they got to the cabin, they'd want the scene as pristine as possible and she didn't want to do anything that might compromise evidence. But she found nothing tying Ashley to the place.

Meanwhile, the whole time she searched, Payton Penn repeated the same word over and over like a mantra: "Lawyer."

Eventually she decided to take him in, but not to Pacific Division, which was a two-hour drive and had an angry lieutenant waiting to confiscate her badge and gun. Nothing that had happened at the cabin was likely to change Hillman's mind about that. She called the Twin Peaks substation of the San Bernardino Sheriff's Department to let them know they'd be having visitors.

As she did a more thorough body check of Payton Penn before walking him down the hill, she discovered a phone in his pocket. It was emitting a soft beeping noise every three seconds.

"What's this?" she asked.

"Lawyer," he answered.

Keri tossed it on the couch in frustration.

"Seriously," he said, "it's an alert beacon that goes out to my lawyer. I pushed it while you were illegally searching my home. Since I don't trust you to let me contact him, I did it myself. So if you're thinking of roughing me up any more, just know that my attorney will be here soon."

"What kind of person has an alert beacon on his phone to reach his lawyer? It's like the bat signal for assholes."

"Lawyer," Payton Penn said, returning to his non-cooperative ways.

Keri left the phone on the couch as they headed down the hill. If the lawyer was tracking it, he'd at least be delayed a bit.

*

Keri was frustrated. As she sat in the Twin Peaks substation two hours after arresting Payton Penn, she was no closer to finding Ashley than she'd been when she busted through that cabin door.

She had tried to question him multiple times through the small cell in the corner of the room but he just kept saying "lawyer" and repeating a phone number with a 213 area code. That meant his lawyer was based in downtown Los Angeles and not some local bumpkin. The sheriff, a man named Courson, must have realized that too because he eventually pulled Keri aside and told her he had no choice but to call the number. They didn't want a civil rights violation lawsuit from some rich LA attorney. They couldn't afford it.

Then he gave her even worse news. He'd contacted her boss at Pacific Division to read him in, a guy named Hillman, who wanted her to call in immediately. The sheriff told her she could videoconference from his office, where she'd have some privacy. She thanked him and reluctantly made the call from the sheriff's surprisingly hi-tech video set-up.

Hillman and Ray popped up on the screen. She was at least glad it wasn't the whole squad.

"Care to explain yourself?" Hillman asked. She launched in.

"Sir, Payton Penn has a motive to abduct Ashley. His own brother suspects that the threatening letter they received came from him. And that note in the van everyone was so sure Ashley wrote could have been forged. Payton stayed with his brother's family last spring. Mia told me he wasn't supervised. He could have easily gotten the stationery from Ashley's room. He could have taken things she'd written and used them to trace a note that credibly looked like her handwriting. If he's been planning this for a while, then he'd have lots of time to get it right."

To her surprise, neither man spoke.

"What is it?" she asked.

Hillman looked almost sheepish as he spoke.

"About that—the FBI tells me that they've started preliminary analysis on the note from Ashley and they've found some…anomalies."

"What does that mean?"

"It means they're no longer certain she wrote it."

Ashley tried not to gloat but couldn't resist one little dig.

"Do you still want my gun and badge?"

The sheepishness disappeared from Hillman's face.

"Don't get cocky, Locke. We both know your phone didn't cut out earlier. Besides, my understanding is that you didn't find anything incriminating at the cabin."

"I only got to do a cursory search. I need to go back and do a more thorough one."

"And you will, once we get a warrant."

"Exigent circumstances, sir."

"When you first busted in, maybe. But that won't fly anymore. We need to do this by the book from here on out. Give us an hour or two down here and we'll have the paperwork sorted out. You can wait at the station up there and lead the search once we get approval. I'm sending Sands up to assist. He should be there by the time we get the warrant authorized."

Ray shifted uncomfortably beside Hillman but said nothing. Sheriff Courson poked his head into the office.

"Penn's lawyer is here," he said. Keri nodded.

"I've got to go," she told Hillman.

"Okay. But you're not to take any further action without authorization. Is that understood?"

"Yes sir," she said before hanging up and returning to the station bullpen.

Even before the sheriff introduced him, Keri was put off by the lawyer. On the surface, he was attractive. His jet black hair was slicked back like some 1980s Wall Street warrior. He had a broad smile that vaguely reminded her of the Joker from the Batman movies. His teeth were unnaturally white and his skin was unnaturally tan. His suit probably cost upwards of five thousand dollars. Almost everything about him oozed insincerity. Everything, that is, except his eyes, which were bright and alert and currently focused on her.

"Detective Keri Locke," said Sheriff Courson, "this is Mr. Penn's attorney, Jackson Cave."

Cave stepped toward her and extended his hand. Keri forced herself not to react visibly even though every nerve ending was on edge. This was the man who could potentially lead her to the Collector and maybe even to Evie.

"Nice to meet you, Detective," he said as he clasped her hand between both of his and gave her that cheesy political handshake that was so common these days. "I've been hearing a lot about you lately."

"Right back at you, Counselor," she said, staring at him unblinkingly.

"Oh, that's intriguing," he said, seemingly genuinely curious. "Perhaps we could get a drink sometime and swap war stories, somewhere a little less…rustic."

Out of the corner of her eye, Keri could see that Sheriff Courson appreciated Jackson Cave about as much as she did.

"Don't hold your breath."

"No, of course not. And I suggest you don't hold your breath when it comes to keeping my client locked up much longer. He'll be making bail in the next few hours, just as soon as we return to an LA courtroom and show a judge video footage of Mr. Penn at work all day yesterday, including the exact time of his niece's alleged abduction. It would seem that you wasted a trip up here on a wild goose chase, Detective."

"I wouldn't call it a waste, Mr. Cave. After all, I got to meet you. And I have a feeling we'll be running into each other again."

She nodded at Sheriff Courson and he followed her into his office.

"Sheriff, I need to ask you a favor."

"What's that?"

"Can you drag this thing out as long as possible? Don't offer to drive Penn back to LA. Demand that LAPD or the County Sheriff come up and take custody. Take your time with the paperwork. In general, drag your heels. I need time to get ahead of this case before that asshole Cave starts mucking everything up. A girl's life may depend on it."

"Frankly, Detective, I was inclined to do all that on my own. Payton Penn has been a pain in my rear for years and his lawyer hasn't endeared himself to me much either."

"Great. Can I leave here directly from your office? The longer it takes before Cave realizes I'm gone, the more of a head start I can get."

"The door's right there," he said.

Keri didn't need to be told twice.

*

She called Ray from the car on the way back out to Payton Penn's place.

"I'm going back up to the cabin," she told him, skipping the pleasantries entirely.

"Nice to speak with you too, partner," he said, clearly as annoyed with her as she was with him. "Don't do something dumb,

Keri. I'm on my way up there now. We'll have the warrant soon. Just wait it out."

"Ashley could be dead by then."

"We're still not even a hundred percent sure she was abducted at all, much less by this guy."

"Raymond, would you rather be overly aggressive and be wrong or too lax and be wrong? If I'm wrong, the worst that happens is I get fired or sued. But if she was taken and we slow boat this, a girl could end up dead. It's not a tough call."

"Okay, but what if he is the guy and you find something without a warrant? It might be inadmissible in court."

"I've got latex gloves and I'll be careful not to leave any traces. I was already in the place once to arrest him. So finding my DNA won't be a shock."

"Is there anything I can say to get you to hold off?" he pleaded.

"You can tell me Ashley Penn was just discovered safe and sound. Short of that, no."

She heard Ray sigh heavily.

"I'll be up there in about ninety minutes. Please be careful."

"You got it, Godzilla."

CHAPTER TWENTY SEVEN

Tuesday
Late Morning

When she came to, the first thing Ashley felt was pain. It was so intense that at first she couldn't identify where it was coming from. Part of her was too afraid to open her eyes and check. She knew she was lying on her back at least. But other than that everything was hazy. She didn't have any idea how long she'd been out.

She took a deep breath and forced her eyes open. The first thing she noticed was that she'd landed pretty squarely in the middle of the padded area she'd created using the mattress. The second thing she noticed was that her head was screaming in pain. Her body may have hit the ground first but clearly the back of her head did too. There was blood everywhere.

She glanced at her aching left hand and saw that the wrist was bent unnaturally. It was clearly broken. Her right leg also throbbed. She tilted her head to get a better look. Something was definitely wrong with her shin. The whole lower leg area was swollen up to about the size of a football. She shifted her weight and involuntarily screamed out in pain. Her tail bone felt like it had cracked in half. If that's what she landed on, it probably did.

Ashley forced herself to crawl toward the door of the silo. Every move sent stabs of pain throughout her body. Through her watery eyes, she saw what looked like a reconfigured examination table in a corner. There were straps on the sides and a head restraint. She decided not to think about what it might be used for.

There was a small desk and chair by the door, which she used to pull herself up. She sat gingerly on the edge of the desk as she caught her breath. It was brutally hot at the base of the silo and her nearly naked body was slick with peanut butter, sweat, and blood. She realized the clothes she'd tossed down the funnel were still over on the clump of padding but there was no way she could make it back to get them.

She reached for the door handle and a terrible thought occurred to her.

What if I've gone through all this and the door is locked from the outside?

She started to laugh, aware that she was slightly hysterical but unable to stop. Eventually she calmed back down, grabbed the handle, and pushed.

It opened. Sunlight flooded in, temporarily blinding her. When her eyes adjusted, she took a moment to assess the area. Outside, everything was quiet and normal. A bird flew by as a gentle breeze ruffled her hair. About a hundred yards away stood an old farmhouse. Behind it was a dilapidated barn. Both were surrounded by barren fields that hadn't had crops in years.

She grabbed the chair and headed in the opposite direction, down a rutted dirt road choked with weeds and foliage. She used the chair as a kind of walker, limping on her left leg as she braced herself with her right hand and left forearm. She turned it around and sat when she needed a break.

She followed the road to the top of a sloping hill. When she got there, what she saw made her want to cry out in joy. There was a paved road about two hundred yards off in the distance. It was a long way but if she could make it, then she could flag down some help.

Suddenly she heard the unmistakable sound of a car. Rounding the corner was a silver convertible sedan. Two young women, probably only a few years older than her, sat in the front.

Without thinking, she called out to them.

"Hey! Over here! Help me! Please!"

She waved her one good arm desperately. They would have been too far away to hear her anyway, but as the car passed by she heard music blasting from the speakers. They never even looked her way.

Silence returned to the farm. Then she heard a loud bang, like a screen door slamming shut. She looked in the direction of the farmhouse. A man stood in front of it. He was using his hand to shield his eyes as he scoured the horizon.

Ashley, realizing she was at the top of a hill, immediately dropped to the ground and lay flat. She grabbed at a leg of the chair, trying to pull it onto its side, but the effort required was massive and it took a good ten seconds before it toppled over.

She waited, panting quietly, hoping against hope.

Then, in the distance, she heard a car door close and an engine turn over. It revved as the vehicle picked up speed. It was getting closer. She rolled down the other side of the hill as best she could, ignoring the pain, trying to get as far as possible from the dirt road.

The vehicle stopped. It idled as a door opened and then closed. She heard footsteps getting closer. A figure appeared at the top of the hill but the sun was in her eyes and she couldn't make it out. He stepped forward, blocking out the rays.

"Howdy there," he said amiably.

Memories she'd blocked out flooded into Ashley's brain quicker than she could process them. She recognized the man. He was the guy she'd seen two nights ago at the convenience store near school. She remembered him flirting with her and how she was flattered because he was cute and probably in his early thirties. His name was Alan. She'd even have given him her number if not for Walker. And he was the same guy who'd pulled up next to her in a black van after school yesterday afternoon. She'd only had a second to register that it was him before everything went dark. That was the last thing she remembered before waking up in the silo.

And now he was standing over her, the man who'd kidnapped her, greeting her warmly, as if he didn't have a care in the world.

"You don't look so great," he said as he approached her. "You're all bloody. Your wrist and leg look pretty bad. And my goodness, you're half naked. We should really get you back inside and take a look at you. Then we can resume the experiments."

As he moved closer, even though she knew no one could hear her, Ashley began to scream.

CHAPTER TWENTY EIGHT

Tuesday
Noon

Keri put on her latex gloves and stepped into Payton Penn's cabin for the second time today. She walked the surrounding property before coming in, on the off chance that Ashley was being held in some belowground alternate location. She found nothing.

That didn't surprise her. With his airtight alibi, there was no way Penn could have taken Ashley himself, which meant he had to have help. And if he didn't want to personally get his hands dirty, it made no sense to have her brought back to his own home. She was being held somewhere else.

That's why the first thing she did upon entering the cabin was open the outdated laptop sitting on the coffee table. The dust that had accumulated on it made her nervous. That meant it hadn't been used in a while. One would have expected him to keep in touch with his partner regularly.

A quick search showed that the internet history had been cleared. Not suspicious on its own. But in context it added to her misgivings.

Why does a guy who lives alone in an isolated cabin clear his history? It's not like he has to hide porn from anyone. So what is he hiding?

She went to his bookmarks and pulled up his Yahoo email account. For a guy who was so cautious about his search history, he was pretty sloppy with this. He hadn't logged out the last time he'd been online so the page loaded directly to his inbox rather than requiring a password. Keri did a few quick searches—"abduct," "niece," "Penn"—no luck. She thought for a moment, then tried "van." An email popped up with the username bambamrider22487. She searched for any others with that name and hit the jackpot.

The first one was from bambamrider22487 a month ago and read:

> Re: The Big Game:
> *Per our mutual friend, I have agreed to sell you my ticket. It will cost you $20. It will be waiting for you under seat 21, top deck section 13 at Dodger Stadium this Thursday night. If you take*

*it, I will assume you want to attend and that the
price is right.*

Payton, under the username PPHeeHee, replied:

Will be there.

The next correspondence was two weeks later, from Payton
Penn to bambamrider22487. It read:

*Per your request, I have a van for the game. It is
in the recommended lot. Keys taped to driver side
front inner tire.*

The next correspondence was a week ago, from
bambamrider22487 to Payton Penn:

*The game is a week from today. 1500-West.
Please confirm. This will be last chance to skip
attending.*

Payton replied an hour later:

Confirmed.

Some of it was easy to figure out. The big game was obviously
the abduction. She suspected that the $20 price meant $20,000 to
take Ashley. The van was self-explanatory. 1500-West was almost
certainly military time for 3 PM at West Venice High.

But if Payton was at the Dodgers game, he already had a ticket.
So what was the "ticket" left under the seat? Then it hit her. There
was something in one of the emails saying "Per your request, I have
a van for the game."

But there hadn't been any email correspondence requesting a
van. It must have come verbally. The "ticket" was a phone, most
likely a burner. Keri glanced at Payton's cell phone lying on the
couch where she'd tossed it earlier. It was a fancy Android—
definitely not a burner. That meant the other one was somewhere
else in the house, probably well hidden considering its sensitive
nature.

Keri closed the laptop and looked around the room. She tried to
put herself in Payton Penn's shoes. Where would he hide the
phone?

He's careful enough to know it needs to be hidden. He cleared his search history. But he also left his e-mail accessible. He was smart enough to put some kind of emergency call beacon on his phone to reach his lawyer. But he also admitted that to me. This man is a combination of paranoid, sloppy, lazy, and cocky. Where would a guy like that leave his phone?

It occurred to her that he'd want it easily accessible wherever he was in the small cabin but not personally on him. It was probably in this room. As her eyes scanned her surroundings, Keri imagined Payton rushing over to grab the ringing phone, hoping to get to it before it went to voicemail.

Close but not too close.

And then her eyes fell on the one item in the cabin that didn't look like it belonged to Payton Penn. On the mantel above the fireplace, between an empty beer can and an empty DVD case for something called *Barely Legal: Volume 23*, was a small antique clock, about the size of a tissue box, with ornate Roman numerals on the face. It didn't strike Keri as Payton's style. In addition, it read 6:37 and the time right now was 12:09.

She walked over and picked it up. It was much lighter than she expected and she could hear a rattle inside. She felt around the edges until her finger brushed against a small indentation in the wood on the bottom. She pushed it and the entire underside of the clock popped off. Inside was a small cubby holding a cheap flip phone.

Keri took it out and looked at the call log. Starting three weeks ago, several calls came to Payton from different phone numbers. She dialed them one by one. The first one was a payphone. The second one was a different payphone; same for the third, and the fourth. Then, on the seventh number, after six rings, the call went to a brief voicemail.

"Leave a message." The voice was bland and unremarkable, but Keri knew this had to be Ashley's abductor. She put all the numbers in her own phone, carefully returned Payton's to the clock, put it back on the mantel, and left the cabin.

Once back in her car and driving down Payton's endless driveway, she made three calls. The first was to Detective Edgerton, back at the station. He was the tech guru of the unit. She gave him all the numbers and asked him to trace their locations. She also gave him the Yahoo user name "bambamrider22487." She was almost certain it was an anonymous account. This guy was much more careful than Payton. Then she put Edgerton on hold while she called Sheriff Courson. She kept it short and to the point.

"Sheriff, I'm headed out of town but I realized no one has secured Payton Penn's cabin. Our CSU team won't be there for another hour or so. I would hate for anyone, say a fancy LA lawyer, to head out there and 'clean up' the place. Maybe you could have one of your people secure it until our team gets there."

"I think that's a wonderful idea, Detective," Courson agreed. "We'll have someone out there in ten minutes.

"Thank you," she said before switching back to Edgerton, who was ready with the information she needed.

Her next call was to Ray but it went straight to voicemail. That wasn't a shock as he was probably making his way up through the mountains to Twin Peaks right now and in an area with limited service. She left a message anyway.

"Ray. I hope you get this soon. Payton Penn *is* involved. I found e-mails between him and a hired kidnapper in the cabin. I also found a burner phone with numbers in the log. Edgerton traced them for me. The last one had an address and a name—Alan Jack Pachanga, thirty-two. He's been in and out of lockup since he was a teenager, mostly for assault, armed robbery, and other good stuff. But he's stayed off the radar for the last couple of years. He lives on a farm near Acton. Edgerton can give you the exact details if you call him. I'm headed there now. At this time of day, with sirens, I figure it'll take me a little over an hour. Maybe you want to join me? I'll try to hold off until you get there. But you know me, always doing something dumb."

She hung up and tossed the phone on the passenger seat, realizing she must still be a little pissed at her partner for not backing her up earlier. Or was there something more to it?

She pushed the thought out of her head. They'd work out their issues later.

As Keri pulled onto Highway 138 and headed west, she put the siren on her roof and gunned the accelerator, going as fast as the mountain road would allow.

Hold on, Ashley. I'm coming.

CHAPTER TWENTY NINE

Tuesday
Early Afternoon

The quickest way to Acton from Twin Peaks was to take Highway 138 west as it cut through and skirted just north of the Angeles National Forest. Much of the way was only two lanes but with her siren on, drivers pulled quickly to the side and she was able to make decent time. In just over an hour she had merged with Highway 14 in the Antelope Valley and was nearing the outskirts of Acton, where Pachanga's farm was located.

She passed the entrance to the place, which was gated and locked with a chain, and drove another quarter mile before turning around. She pulled off the road about a hundred yards from the farm and eased the Prius along the dirt shoulder, settling behind an overgrown high patch of bushes that would hide it pretty well unless someone got close.

She got out her binoculars and tried to get a sense of the farm. Unfortunately, the dirt road—more of a trail really—led up a hill and she couldn't see what was on the other side of the rise.

She grabbed her phone to call Ray, whom she hadn't heard from. Only then did she realize why. Now she didn't have cell service. It wasn't really a shock so far out. In retrospect, she should have called him when she was passing near Palmdale, where she surely would have had reception.

She noticed the blinking envelope icon and realized she had a text, although she hadn't heard it come in. It was from Ray and read:

"Arrived Twin Peaks. Got your message. En route to farm. Don't be stupid. Wait for me."

The timestamp was 1:03, about a half hour ago. If he drove as quickly as she did, he would arrive in about thirty minutes, at just after two. Could she wait that long?

Keri's thoughts went to Jackson Cave. Payton Penn had obviously spoken to him. What if he'd told Cave to contact Pachanga and tell him that capture was imminent and he should dispose of any evidence of their crime, including Ashley? It wasn't a far-fetched concern. If that had happened, she might already be too late. Waiting another half hour would be irresponsible.

She had no choice.

She had to go in.

150

*

Keri grabbed her gun and binoculars, put on her bulletproof vest and a pair of sunglasses, and walked across the quiet road to Pachanga's property.

Arriving at the gate to the farm, Keri noted that while it and the chain were rusted over, the padlock for them was shiny and brand new. A grungy sign read:

Private Property.
No Trespassing.

Rather than try to climb over it, she shimmied between the barbed wire fencing that ran along the entire property and started up the hill. She didn't walk on the road itself, in case a car suddenly appeared, but about ten yards next to it, where she could drop into the dense shrubbery to hide.

When she neared the top of the hill, Keri got on her stomach and crawled the rest of the way. She poked her head up and saw the entire area.

At one time, it must have been a working farm. There were marked fields, a grain silo, a barn, and a farmhouse. But it clearly hadn't been used for that purpose in many years. The fields were littered with weeds and several old tractors, silently standing guard. It fact, multiple rusted-out vehicles dotted the property. None appeared to be operational. The barn looked to be falling apart. And the silo was rusted over. A dry creek bed cut the middle of the property in half.

There wasn't much cover for her to get down the hill and look around. She'd have to crawl another fifty yards through the brush before reaching a wooded area that ran along the creek to the farmhouse. From there she could use some of the trees and abandoned cars to hide her approach to the silo and the barn. It would be slow going but she could do it.

She checked her phone one last time—still no signal. She put it on silent as a precaution, slid the binoculars into her pocket, and started down the hill.

Ten minutes later, she reached the farmhouse. The front door was shut and locked. She circled the house, crouching, peering into windows, but didn't see any movement. She headed for the barn, darting behind a wheel-less station wagon and several trees along the way.

She reached the entrance and looked in. She didn't see anyone but in the middle of the barn, right below the hayloft, was a shiny red pickup truck.

Pachanga must be here somewhere!

He must have put the vehicle here in the barn to keep it hidden from the road. She carefully made her way over to it and looked in the open window. The keys were in the ignition.

Keri quietly pulled them out and shoved them in her pants pocket. At least now, if she found Ashley, she had a way to get her out. And unless one of those tractors could be fired up, Pachanga wouldn't have a way to follow.

A loud metal banging sound shook her out her self-congratulatory daydream.

She hurried back out and around the barn to see where it had come from.

A man was working his way down the ladder fixed on the side of the silo. The sound must have been him closing the hatch at the top. She couldn't see his face but his hair was sun-bleached blond. He wore jeans, work boots and a white T-shirt that contrasted with his deeply tanned skin. From what Keri could tell, he wasn't especially tall, maybe five-ten. But his frame was thick and muscular. She guessed he weighed over 200 pounds and his biceps burst against the sleeves of his shirt.

Keri couldn't help but wonder if this was the Collector. Was this the man who had taken Evie? He was blond and she had thought she saw blond hair under the cap of Evie's abductor. But that man had a tattoo on his neck and Pachanga clearly didn't.

Of course, hair could be changed and tattoos removed. But something didn't match. This guy looked to be younger, somewhere around thirty. So he would have been in his mid-twenties when Evie was taken. But Keri remembered there were wrinkles near the outside of the other man's eyes—a detail she hadn't recalled until this very moment. Evie's abductor was probably forty or older.

Keri felt herself sliding into one of her mournful reveries and shook herself out of it. This wasn't the time or the place. She had a job to do and she couldn't afford to have a grief blackout right now.

Pachanga reached the bottom of the ladder and turned around, wiping the sweat from his brow with his forearm. Keri was stunned at how handsome he was. He had azure blue eyes and a crooked smile. It wasn't hard to imagine Ashley approaching the van just to get a closer look at him.

Pachanga glanced around the property for a moment, then disappeared into the base of the silo through a metal door that he closed behind him.

Keri moved quickly through the trees until she was just outside the door. There were no windows in the silo and she was pretty sure she couldn't be detected. She placed her ear to the door and slowed her breathing so it wouldn't interfere with her hearing.

She could identify a voice. It was male and the words were low and calm. She couldn't understand what he was saying but he sounded almost playful. Then she heard another voice—louder, scared and female. She was mostly whimpering but spoke intermittently. Her words were slurred, like she'd been drugged. Keri couldn't understand much of what she said. But two were clear:

"Please! No!"

Keri checked her weapon, removed the safety, took a long, slow, deep breath, and then quietly and slowly turned the door handle. She pulled the door open just enough to peek inside. She could hardly believe her eyes.

Ashley Penn was lying on what looked to be a doctor's examination table, propped up forty-five degrees at the head. Her legs were strapped into stirrups and her arms were stretched down to the base of the table with leather straps. Her head was stuck in some kind of vise that prevented her from moving it. She was wearing only panties and a bra and her entire body was caked in blood and some brown substance. Something was wrong with her left wrist, which hung limply in its strap. Her right lower leg also looked bad. It was a deep purple and horribly swollen. A device next to the table beeped and Keri saw each strap tighten and pull on Ashley's limbs about a half inch. She screamed in pain.

It's like some automated version of the medieval rack. If this goes on much longer, her arms and legs will be ripped from her body.

Keri forced herself not to run right over to the girl. There was no sign of Pachanga. Keri poked her head around the door to see if he was hiding behind it—nothing. Then she noticed another door a few feet behind the table. It was slightly ajar. He must have gone in there.

Keri looked back at Ashley and saw that the girl was looking directly back at her. Keri put her finger to her lips to indicate silence and stepped inside. Ashley seemed to be desperately trying to form a word without success. Keri glanced at the little table by the door and noticed a small black-and-white monitor on it.

As she stared at it, trying to identify the image on the screen, Ashley managed to blurt out one word:

"Beeyyind!"

Everything after that seemed to happen all at once. Keri realized the monitor was connected to a security camera that was trained on the main silo door. And as she processed that Pachanga must have seen her on it, Ashley's single word became clear in her head.

Behind!

At that moment, on the monitor, she saw an image flash into view and realized it was Alan Jack Pachanga—and that he was right behind her.

CHAPTER THIRTY

Tuesday
Early Afternoon

Keri saw the lead pipe in Pachanga's hands on the monitor. He was holding it overhead, preparing to swing it down toward her gun hand, hoping to knock the weapon loose and shatter her forearm in the process.

She spun quickly to her right. The pipe came down hard where her hand used to be but now it was her left shoulder there. She felt a crunch as her collarbone gave way. She fell backward to the ground, screaming in pain, temporarily blinded by bright white flashes of agony.

As her vision cleared, she saw Pachanga bearing down on her, only steps away. She raised her right hand and fired. His howl told her she'd hit him but she wasn't sure where. He collapsed on top of her and rolled to the floor beside her. For half a second she thought he was dead.

But he wasn't. She saw him clutching at his right leg and realized she'd hit him in the upper thigh. She pulled the gun across her body to take a second shot. But he saw her move, grabbed the pipe, and swung it at her, knocking it out of her hand along with the pipe. Both went flying off across the silo floor and stopped under the table Ashley was lying on.

Pachanga leapt at her. Before Keri could stop him, the man had grabbed her arms, pinned them to the ground, and was climbing on top of her. He was unbelievably strong.

"Nice to meet you, ma'am. Sorry it's under less than preferable circumstances," he said before punching her in the face.

Keri felt her eye socket crack and once again a shower of light exploded in her brain. She prepared for a second punch but it didn't come. Another scream from the corner of the room told Keri that Ashley's limbs had been pulled another half inch apart. She looked up through watery eyes to see Pachanga smiling down at her.

"You know, you're real pretty for a lady of your advanced years. I was supposed to keep the specimen over there unsullied for negotiating purposes. I could only do limited experiments. But I don't have any such limitations with you. I think I may have to make you my special experiment, if you know what I mean. Do you know what I mean?"

Amazingly, he was smiling warmly, as if he'd just asked her out for a cup of coffee. Keri didn't respond, which seemed to make him unhappy. His wide grin twisted into an ugly grimace. Without warning he reared back and punched Keri in the rib, the very same one that was already throbbing from her struggle with Johnnie Cotton.

If it wasn't broken before, it definitely was now. Keri gasped for air, so shot through with pain that she didn't know where to focus. She could hear Pachanga talking but his words were drowned out by the roar of anguish in her own head.

"...gonna get to see my True Self. Not many specimens have had the privilege. But I can tell you're special. You found my Home Base all on your own. That must mean you chose to be here with me. I'm flattered."

Keri feared she was going to pass out. If that happened, it was over. She had to do something fast to change the dynamic. Pachanga was prattling on in some kind of delusional ecstasy, talking about home bases and true selves. She didn't have a clue what he was talking about. His eyes were bright with madness and he was drooling slightly. He seemed oblivious to his leg wound, which was bleeding profusely. The wound—she had an idea.

"Hey," she said, interrupting his speech. "Why don't you shut it, you pathetic little loser."

The rapturous fervor in his eyes disappeared, replaced by fury.

He raised his fist above his head again, ready to pummel her once more. But this time when he did, Keri dug her thumb hard into his bullet wound. He fell off her to the ground. Keri was prepared for that and rolled with him, keeping her thumb in the hole in his flesh, digging hard, rooting around, refusing to break contact. With her left hand, she pulled the pickup truck keys from her pocket, bunched them together and, ignoring the lightning bolt of pain that rocked her from shoulder to fingertip, jabbed down hard at Pachanga's face. She got him once in the cheek, ripping a gaping hole in it, and once in the left eye before he managed to break free and scramble away.

As he did, Keri used the table to pull herself to her feet. She looked at her assailant. He was curled up in a ball, his hands to his face, blood pouring through his fingers. She started to make a move toward the gun but as she did, Pachanga dropped his hands and stared at her with his one working eye. He knew what she was after and he wasn't going to let her get to it. Ashley screamed again as the machine stretched her limbs once more.

There were no good choices here so Keri made the only one she could. She turned and ran out the silo door.

*

She waited until she'd made it about fifty yards before glancing back at the silo. She knew she'd never be able to reach the gun. Her only chance to save Ashley and herself was to draw Pachanga away from the girl; to keep his focus on her.

When she looked around, he was nowhere in sight.

Oh God, it didn't work. He's staying with her. He's going to kill her.

She had to do something.

"Hey, Alan," she yelled, "what's wrong? You giving up? Can't handle a real woman? Don't know what to do unless they're tied down? I guess we're seeing your True Self now. And it looks like he's a wuss."

She stood there, waiting for some response, praying for some kind of reaction. Nothing. He wasn't biting.

And then he was in the doorway. He leaned against it for support. He'd taken off his T-shirt and tied it around his leg wound. There was nothing he could do about his face, which was a mask of blood on the left side and mostly clean on the right. He looked like Halloween come to life.

He stumbled after her, lumbering slowly but with purpose. She staggered ahead of him toward the barn, ignoring her shoulder and her ribs and her face, all of which throbbed remorselessly. When she reached the barn she turned around again.

"Come on, lover," she shouted, "don't you want me? You can't make me scream if you can't catch me. I thought you were supposed to be in charge, big boy. But you seem like a little weakling to me."

Pachanga stopped for second beside an old sedan, resting his arm on it to keep from falling. Keri thought he was going to say something. Instead, he pulled a gun—her gun—out from the back of his waistband and aimed it at her.

That must have been what took him so long to come out of the silo. He'd gone back for her gun. He aimed it at her and fired. She darted safely behind the side of the barn and rushed inside. She got into the pickup truck and fumbled for the key before finally managing to shove it in the ignition. She turned it and felt a wave of relief as it roared to life.

Her left arm was mostly useless so she had to reach across her body to close the door. She put the car in drive, hit the accelerator, and smashed thought the back wall of the barn in the direction she'd last seen Pachanga.

She'd hoped he was close enough that she could just run him over. But he was moving slowly and was still a good thirty yards away. She steered directly at him and punched the gas hard.

Pachanga lifted her gun and started firing. The first shot shattered the windshield. Keri ducked but kept driving. She heard more shots but couldn't tell where they went. Then there was a loud pop and she knew a bullet had hit one of the tires. She felt the truck careen to the right toward the creek bed, then roll over. She lost track of how many times it rolled before coming to a stop.

Keri tried to orient herself. Eventually she figured out that the truck had landed on the driver's side and Keri was lying on the door. She could see the blue sky through the passenger window.

She had no idea if the pain she felt was from new injuries she'd sustained in the crash or old ones. It all blended together. She pulled herself up so that she was upright, standing on the driver's side door. She reached for the passenger window but something yanked her back. She looked down and saw her foot was trapped under the brake pedal. She tried to wriggle herself free but without the use of her left arm, it was impossible. She was trapped.

Suddenly Pachanga's face appeared in the open passenger window. Before Keri could react, he swung a chain around her neck, twisted, and yanked it tight. Keri gasped for breath. She tried to slump down but he yanked her up again.

"I thought about using the gun but decided this would be more fun," he said, unconcerned about the loose chunk of his cheek that flapped when he spoke.

Keri tried to speak, hoping that if she could bait him, he'd drop the chain and try to come in the truck after her. But no words came out.

"You're done talking, ma'am," Pachanga growled, all pretense of charm now gone. "You'll be unconscious in a few more seconds. And then I'm taking you back to Home Base where I'm going to do things to you that will make you wish you were dead."

Keri tried to get her fingers under the chain but it was too tight. She could feel blackness starting to envelop her. In one futile effort to fight back, she pressed her knee against the steering wheel horn, hoping the blaring would startle him. It didn't. Still, she pressed on it, her last little bit of rebellion.

The blue sky turned gray and everything went tingly. The light faded. Keri's eyelids fluttered. Out of the corner of her eye, she thought she saw the shadow of a bird pass overhead. She heard a grunt. And then there was only blackness.

*

When Keri came to, she realized she must have only been out very briefly. Her knee was still on the horn. The pressure on her neck was gone. In fact, the chain hung loosely and she was able to pull it off. She heard noises above but couldn't identify them.

And then suddenly two bodies slammed onto the truck above her. Pachanga was on the bottom, squirming to get free. But someone was top of him, pinning him down and repeatedly punching him with blows to the face, the body, the face again.

It was Ray.

He continued to punch until Pachanga lay still. His head slumped to the side and smushed against the truck's rear window. He was unconscious.

Ray stood up, stared at the man below him, then kicked him in the stomach. Pachanga remained silent.

Ray looked down into the cab of the truck at Keri.

"You okay?" he asked.

"I've been better," she replied, her voice raw and raspy.

"I told you to wait for me," he said sternly but with a smile playing at his lips. Keri was about to respond when a loud scream pierced the air.

"It's Ashley. She's tied to some kind of rack in that silo. It's going to rip her limbs off. You've got to get to her now!"

"What about this guy?" he asked, nodding at Pachanga.

"I don't think he's going to be much trouble. Just get to Ashley. Now! I'm okay here."

Ray nodded and disappeared from view.

Keri slumped to the bottom of the cab and closed her eyes.

A few minutes later, Ashley's screams finally stopped. Ray had gotten to her.

Keri slowly opened her eyes. The world rushed back in and with it, all the pain. She tried to shut it out by focusing her attention on getting her foot free from under the car brake. It took a minute but she was able to ease it out. She pulled herself up, preparing for the next big task—climbing out of the truck. She looked up, searching for the best handholds to grab. Immediately she saw that something was wrong.

Pachanga was gone.

Trying to stay calm, Keri wedged her body against the back window of the cab and put her feet on the dashboard, creating enough tension to inch her way up. Eventually, she got high enough to hook her right arm around the passenger side view mirror. Her left arm still lay limp at her side so she stepped onto the steering wheel and pushed off while she yanked on the mirror. The combined force got the upper half of her body out of the truck. She looked around.

In the distance she saw Pachanga limping clumsily toward the silo. He was almost to the door. In his right hand was Keri's gun.

She tried to shout out but her voice was still hoarse from being strangled.

He disappeared inside. Five endless seconds later, a gunshot rang through the air.

Keri wriggled her lower half out of the truck and got to her feet. She ran toward the silo, ignoring every throbbing part of her body, ignoring the fact that even breathing was difficult.

As she ran by the sedan that Pachanga had stopped to lean on, she saw a crowbar in the brown grass by the trunk. She bent down, clutched it in her working right hand, and continued toward the silo.

When she approached the open door, she wanted to burst in but forced herself to take it slow. Remembering the security camera, she looked around and saw it perched on an exposed beam, facing away from her location.

She hurried around behind the silo, hoping that the back door Pachanga had left open earlier was still ajar. It was. She stole a quick look inside.

It was bad.

Ray sat slumped against the wall, blood seeping from a wound in his gut. She couldn't tell if he was alive or dead.

He had clearly freed Ashley but now Pachanga was strapping her back onto the table. She was fighting desperately but losing the battle. He had all her limbs but her right leg strapped down. The gun was nestled in his waistband.

Keri stepped forward, crowbar in hand. Ashley noticed and glanced involuntarily in her direction. Pachanga saw it too and knew something was wrong.

He spun around and pulled the gun out. Keri was still four feet away, too far to lunge at him. He grinned, making the same calculation.

"You are just full of surprises," he muttered, a ghastly smile spreading across his ruined face. "We are going to have so much fun toge—"

With her free leg, Ashley kicked Pachanga directly where he'd been shot in the thigh. He gasped and bent over in pain.

Keri stepped forward immediately, pulled the crowbar back above her head, and then brought the curved end down fast and hard on the top of Alan Jack Pachanga's skull.

He dropped to his knees.

In that moment, Keri knew she could stop, that he would pass out. That it was over.

But she couldn't stop.

She thought of Evie. Of all the monsters like this in the world. Of the scumbag lawyers. Of this man getting out somehow, someday.

And she could not allow that to happen.

She raised the crowbar high, and he looked up at her and grinned, blood seeping from his mouth.

"You won't do it," he muttered.

She brought it down with every ounce of strength she had left—and it lodged in his skull.

Pachanga remained there motionless for several seconds, then collapsed to the floor. Keri's gun fell from his hand and rested at Keri's feet. She picked it up and kept it aimed at him as she rolled him over with her foot. He stared up at her with his one empty azure blue eye.

Alan Jack Pachanga was dead.

Keri heard the soft crying from across the room and she realized something even more startling.

Ashley Penn was alive.

It was over.

CHAPTER THIRTY ONE

Thursday
Mid-morning

Keri lay awake in bed, enjoying the solitude. She knew there would be visitors later but for now she had the room to herself. She tried to piece together the last few days through the haze of sleep and pain medication.

Because Ray Sands had better foresight than Keri, he had called for backup on his way out to the farm. The first officers had arrived fifteen minutes after Keri killed Pachanga and the farm was swarming with cops and EMTs five minutes after that. After stabilizing Ray, who was clinging to life, they got everyone to nearby Palmdale Regional Medical Center less than ten minutes later.

Keri had refused to undergo surgery on her collarbone until doctors informed her that Ray was in surgery himself. He'd lost a lot of blood but they were hopeful he'd pull through.

Most of Wednesday was a blur. She drifted in and out of consciousness but stayed awake long enough to learn that Ray was in serious but stable condition. He was in the ICU. Ashley had a fractured left wrist, a shattered tibia, a cracked coccyx, and a concussion, all from her fall. She also had a dislocated left shoulder as a result of Pachanga's rack device. She was supposedly going to recover from all of them.

For her part, Keri's left arm was in a sling. The doctors said her collarbone was a clean break and that she'd recover in six to eight weeks. She had a cushioned mask on her face, much like the one Ray used in his Olympic boxing days. It was designed to protect her orbital bone from any further damage. She'd have to wear it for at least another week. Her neck was in a brace to protect the muscles that had been strained by the chain. There was nothing they could really do about her broken ribs except pad the area. She had multiple other scrapes and bruises, as well as a concussion of her own. But it all seemed minor in comparison to what had happened to the other two.

A nurse walked in, pushing someone in a wheelchair.

"You have a visitor," she said.

Keri couldn't see who it was while lying down so she pushed the button on her remote to raise her to a seated position.

She was surprised to see that it was Ashley.

Ashley rolled close, then sat there for a while, clearly unsure what to say.

Keri decided to break the ice.

"Looks like it's going to be a while before you're surfing again."

Ashley's face brightened at the thought.

"Yeah," she agreed. "But the doctors say I will eventually get back on the board."

"I'm glad, Ashley."

"I just wanted to…you know…um, you saved my life," she said, tears welling up in her eyes. "I don't really know how to thank you for that." She wiped away the tears with her good hand.

"I know a way you can thank me. Make it matter. Don't let this be a wasted opportunity. You're a teenager and every teenager takes risks. I get that. But you were headed down a dangerous road, Ashley. I've seen lots of girls take the path you were on and not come back. You have a good life. Not a perfect one but a good one. You're smart. You're tough. You have friends. You have a bed to sleep in each night and a mother who would fight off wolves for you. A lot of kids can't say that. And now you've got a fresh start. Please don't waste it."

Ashley nodded. A hug felt appropriate but in their conditions neither was up for it, so smiles had to do. In those smiles, they both said more than they ever could with words. This ordeal had bonded them, a bond Keri sensed would last for life. She would check up on Ashley down the road, and Ashley would stay in touch with her. She knew it.

After the nurse wheeled her away, Keri could not help but think of the other girl she had rescued: Susan Granger.

She summoned a nurse, who helped her call the group home where Susan had been placed. Susan sounded okay, even upbeat. It seemed as if her hearing the news of Ashley's rescue somehow gave her hope for the future, too. Bad guys, she was learning, were not all-powerful after all.

Susan agreed to give Keri another few days before insisting on an in-person visit. Apparently being hospitalized with multiple injuries was a good enough excuse to get a rain check.

About an hour later, Lieutenant Cole Hillman came into the room. Beside him stood Reena Beecher, captain of the entire West LA Division. She was a tall, sinewy woman in her mid-fifties. She had sharp features accentuated by deep lines caused by years of dealing with the worst of humanity. Her blackish-gray hair was tied back in a tight bun. Keri had seen her in the halls but they'd never spoken before. Beecher walked over to the bed.

"How are you feeling, Detective?" she asked.

"Not too bad, Captain. Give me a week and I'll be back on duty."

Beecher chuckled softly.

"Well, we may give you a little longer than that. But I appreciate the attitude. Before the day gets crazy, I just wanted to thank you for your diligence and hard work. If it wasn't for you, Ashley Penn would almost certainly be dead and no one would even be looking for her."

"Thank you, ma'am," Keri said, catching Hillman's annoyed expression out of the corner of her eye.

"However, in the future, you would do well to more fully read in your superiors on what you're doing. I'll be honest—if not for the high-profile nature of this case, you'd be on suspension right now. You understand what I'm saying? No more lone wolf stuff. You've got a partner and a force behind you. Use them. Got it?"

"Yes ma'am. How is my partner, do you know?"

"I'll let Lieutenant Hillman catch you up—on everything." She smiled tightly, patted Keri on the hand, and left the room. Hillman took a seat in the chair in the corner of the room.

"What does all that mean?" Keri asked him. "Catch me up on everything? The day is going to get crazy?"

Hillman sighed deeply.

"First, Ray is doing better. They've been keeping him sedated but they're going to wake him up later this afternoon. You don't have to ask—I've already made accommodations for you to be there. As to the craziness the captain mentioned, there's a press conference scheduled for later today in front of the hospital. The mayor will be there, along with the Penns, Beecher, myself, Chief Donald, and reps from the Sheriff, the FBI, Palmdale PD—and, of course, you."

"Me? I don't want to be there, sir."

"I know. Frankly, neither do I. But we don't really have a choice. You'll be asked to say a few words. You won't have to answer any questions—ongoing investigation and all. Mostly you'll have to sit in a wheelchair for an hour, listening to important people prattle on. Don't ask me to get out of it. It's an order."

"Yes sir," Keri said reluctantly. She didn't yet have the required strength to fight back. "Speaking of the investigation, do you know where we're at?"

"Payton Penn is being held at Twin Towers. With all the evidence they found at his cabin, not even Jackson Cave can bail him out. He'll probably go on trial in the spring. The search of Pachanga's place turned up a lot of evidence of previous abductions. Ashley Penn told them to check the top of the silo. Apparently some of his victims wrote their names on the interior walls. Lots of families are going to get closure this week. They also found a laptop in his farmhouse but so far no one has been able to crack his password. Edgerton's working on it now. In my opinion, he's better than anyone the Feds have. So that's where things stand. I recommend you get some sleep before the press conference."

He got up and went to leave and Keri thought he would go without saying goodbye.

But then he stopped in the doorway, his back to her.

Without turning around, he muttered, reluctantly: "Damn good work, kid."

Then, without another word, he walked away.

Those few words meant more to Keri than she could say.

Keri watched him go, then buzzed again for the nurse, who helped her make another call, this time to Detective Edgerton.

He'd hit a wall trying to access info on the laptop. Apparently it shut down if you entered either the wrong username or password ten times. He was up to eight and was afraid to try again. Keri thought about it for a moment, picturing Pachanga straddling her, his eyes ablaze with manic ecstasy as he preached his unhinged manifesto. Then an idea popped into her head.

"Can I make a suggestion? If I'm wrong, you'll still have one more chance."

"I don't know, Keri," Edgerton said reluctantly.

"Listen. I was with him. He talked to me. He was baring his soul. I'm pretty sure I know this guy."

There came a long silence. Then:

"One guess."

She breathed deep.

"Okay. For the username go with TRUESELF. For the password, use HOMEBASE."

She waited while he typed. There was a long, uncomfortable silence, her heart slamming in her chest, praying she wasn't wrong.

"It worked!" Edgerton shouted. "Oh my God! Holy shit, Keri. This is the mother lode! I'm seeing it now…multiple chat rooms on the dark web…wait a minute, it's loading…that's it! We've got access to them all. Holy shit! This could help break dozens of cases! I've got to let you go so I can concentrate! This is amazing."

She was about to ask him if he saw the name "Collector" anywhere but he'd already hung up. It was probably for the best anyway. She wanted to keep that detail to herself for now.

The nurse hung up the phone for her and lowered the hospital bed. Keri wanted to thank her but she was wiped out and drifted off before getting a word out.

*

The press conference was just as Hillman predicted. Important people blathered on. The Penns thanked her. Mia sounded genuine through her tears. Senator Penn put on a good show but Keri could tell he despised her. Even if she had saved his daughter, his career was in ruins and he seemed to hold her responsible.

Finally she was wheeled up to the microphone.

She'd thought about what she was going to say while she listened to the others. After a while, a plan formed in her mind. She would never have a bigger platform. And she was going to use it.

She started by thanking all the right people and expressing how glad she was that Ashley was okay.

"That young woman fought for herself until others came to help. She showed bravery and toughness and an unrelenting will to survive. In fact, it was her quick thinking that helped save my life. I'm proud of her and I know her parents are too."

Then Keri paused for a second before deciding to go for it. She held up a photo displayed on her phone.

She saw out of the corner of her eyes Hillman shaking his head furiously at her, warning her not to do it.

But nothing would stop her now.

"This is my daughter, Evelyn Locke. We called her Evie. She was abducted five years ago next week when she was just eight years old." Keri swiped the screen to reveal another image. "This an age-progression sketch of what she might look like now at thirteen. I appreciate all the kind words of thanks today. But all I want is my little girl back. So if this image looks familiar, please contact your local authorities. I miss my daughter and just want to hold her again. Please help me do that. Thank you."

She was flooded with a sea of questions, all the attention shifting from the Penns to Evie, and she felt her heart warm.

Maybe they'd find her after all.

*

166

An hour later, Keri sat in a chair at Ray's bedside, waiting for him in the silence to wake up. Her thoughts drifted to what she would do once she was fully recovered. She was toying with the idea of moving out of the houseboat. It was a place for people, she realized, living in a holding pattern. She now realized that. And she felt like she needed to move on if she was going to have any kind of life.

Maybe she'd get an apartment, one with two bedrooms, so Evie would have a place to sleep once she found her. And she'd start seeing Dr. Blanc more regularly. She hadn't had a missing time blackout since the surgery, but she didn't trust that they were gone for good. To make that happen, as much as she hated to admit it, she'd need help.

And maybe it was time to really face up to her feelings for Ray. They'd been doing this delicate dance for a while. She knew he wanted to get closer but she was afraid of letting him in, terrified of allowing herself to truly care for another person who might get ripped away from her. She didn't want to lose him too.

But then it hit her.

We lose everyone eventually. It's what we do with our time here together that matters.

She smiled at the thought, sighing deeply. It was the most relaxed she'd felt in a long time. She glanced up and saw that Ray was conscious and smiling at her, his warm eyes twinkling. She didn't know how long he'd been awake, but the thought of him watching over her gave her comfort.

"How ya doing, Big?" she asked softly.

His voice was weak and raspy but she understood him anyway.

"Better now, Tinkerbell."

Coming Soon!

Book #2 in the Keri Locke mystery series

BOOKS BY BLAKE PIERCE

RILEY PAIGE MYSTERY SERIES
ONCE GONE (Book #1)
ONCE TAKEN (Book #2)
ONCE CRAVED (Book #3)
ONCE LURED (Book #4)
ONCE HUNTED (Book #5)
ONCE PINED (Book #6)

MACKENZIE WHITE MYSTERY SERIES
BEFORE HE KILLS (Book #1)
BEFORE HE SEES (Book #2)
BEFORE HE COVETS (Book #3)

AVERY BLACK MYSTERY SERIES
CAUSE TO KILL (Book #1)
CAUSE TO RUN (Book #2)
CAUSE TO HIDE (Book #3)

KERI LOCKE MYSTERY SERIES
A TRACE OF DEATH (Book #1)

Blake Pierce

Blake Pierce is author of the bestselling RILEY PAGE mystery series, which includes six books (and counting). Blake Pierce is also the author of the MACKENZIE WHITE mystery series, comprising three books (and counting); of the AVERY BLACK mystery series, comprising three books (and counting); and of the new KERI LOCKE mystery series.

An avid reader and lifelong fan of the mystery and thriller genres, Blake loves to hear from you, so please feel free to visit www.blakepierceauthor.com to learn more and stay in touch.

Made in the USA
Coppell, TX
13 April 2022

76501392R00098